The Lamentation of Cin'Céline's
One/None:

The Eye of Eyes

O/N 19

The Lamentation of Cin'Céline's
One/None:

The Eye of Eyes

19

Jan Cichy

Translated from the Polish by Dr. Mirosław Słowik

Introduction by Adam Zmarzlinski

ROMEOVILLE

THE EYE OF EYES ™

Cover art by Lindsey Jachec.
The Lamentation logo, Monotreme Press logo and *One/ None* fragment designed by Cedo Medjed.
'Local Man Flies North' newspaper clipping designed by Cedo Medjed.
Book designed and formatted by Damonza.

ISBN-13: 978-1-951326-03-6 (Paperback)
ISBN-13: 978-1-951326-02-9 (Hardcover)
ISBN-13: 978-1-951326-04-3 (Digital)

Library of Congress Control Number: 2020915855

First printing: September 2021

Monotreme Press
PO Box 7413
Romeoville IL 60446
USA

Visit www.thelamentation.com for more on *The Lamentation of Cin'Céline* and its authors.
Join us on www.monotremepress.com for more.

MP 8 7 6 5 4 3 2 1

For all the weird, eccentric, and peculiar souls that we meet in the dark corners of the world who turn out to be brilliant people glowing with a light of immeasurable kindness and moral will. Mike Arends being one of those radiant spirits.

GLOUCESTER DAILY

February 5, 1901

15

Local Man Flies North

It is a story as old as time, a man goes on a journey. From Odysseus to Robinson Crusoe, Man has struggled to discover and survive. On a chilly February 4th morning, Mr. Jan Cichy, of Snowshill, Gloucestershire, took off in his aero-craft for what he called 'the first latitudinal circumnavigation of the globe.'

Mr. Cichy is a patent officer by trade and an engineer by training. Having come to the Kingdom from Galicia (often referred to as occupied Poland), Mr. Cichy has worked on his aero-craft for the past five years. A first of its kind, the aero-craft, is an odd vehicle: half balloon, half boat. Its inner workings are wires, pipes, and storage space. It is a vehicle taken out of the tales of H. G. Wells or Jules Verne.

While Mr. Cichy's journey has just began, he hopes to return to Snowshill by autumn. He spoke of crossing the two Poles and the Pacific Ocean as the most concerning parts of the charted course. The editors and writers at the Gloucester Daily wish him kind winds and clear skies.

INTRODUCTION

When I began my research, as part of my master's degree in Transatlantic Studies, at Jagiellonian University in 2009, I never thought that I would be rummaging through a treasure throve of ancient documents in the University's Library, a library that, as of this writing, is 655 years old. It all happened, as these things often do, by accident. I was in the middle of researching the symbolism in Emily Dickinson poem, "Because I could not stop for Death." The librarian, a hard-faced middle aged woman, suggested I look at the 1913 copy of the poem found in the Library's Rare Texts section. I needed a letter of permission from a professor to be let in upstairs, where the ominous section was housed. I asked Prof. Laidler for permission, who was kind enough to draft a letter good for a week's worth stay at the Rare Texts section. I went upstairs the very next day, a Saturday.

As I meandered through the shelves and cabinets, each row pungent with rot of ancient papers, I felt at home. After some leisurely searching, I found the Dickinson book. On the next shelf over, between some volumes on Greek poetry and a cardboard file box—where loose papers or crumbling books are often held—sat an unmarked case lacking in a library slip, title, or any spine information whatsoever. Something about it intrigued me, and after grabbing the Dickinson book, I returned to the nameless case and took it with me to my assigned research room.

I opened the case file to find a hundred or so loose sheets blanketed with a great deal of strange markings. I flipped through the pages and read. Captivating, yet nauseating, the tale made me felt uncomfortable. Part fantasy, part horror, all swathed in a veil of social critique, the ramblings of a Jan Cichy made me contemplate reality and the strange human madnesses found within. Hours later, a librarian knocked on the research room door and, rather directly, asked for me to leave. The Library was closing. I thanked her and placed the papers back in the case. I did not get any work done on Dickinson's poem. That was the first time that I had read Jan Cichy's 1901 manuscript, which he titled *Oko Oczu* or *The Eye of Eyes* in English. I jotted down a couple of notes, and returned the case to where I had found it.

Thinking about what I had read made going to sleep challenging. There was so much that I wanted to reread, so much still to ponder. The book read as if it were fiction, yet it was written as a letter to a Jagiellonian University professor, Dr. Michał Nowak, who taught at the school before the start of the First World War. Not able to return to the manuscript until Monday made that Sunday seem longer than usual. I thought of Cichy's description of the black wasteland, of the suicide he had witnessed, of the Eye of Eyes, of the madness inducing sands that charred his soul.

I was the first visitor at the University's Library that Monday morning. With the permission letter in hand, I quickly made my way to the Cichy case, but when I reached the shelf, the manuscript was gone. Between the volumes of Greek poetry and the cardboard file box sat a blank space. I darted between rows looking for it. "Some schmuck must have moved it," I thought. I became angry, until, through the glass door, I saw an elderly bearded man in one of the research rooms. The Cichy manuscript sat spread out before him on the table.

Defeated, I departed the Rare Texts section with a hope that I would get my hands on the manuscript tomorrow. Instead of getting some work done, I decided to find what else the Library held on Jan Cichy. I found a handful of technical texts authored by him: mercury use in thermometers, heat use in ballooning, engine design philosophy, and a few essays that fell under the umbrella of engineering: power systems, geometry in weight distribution, and material science. All these articles gave me an impression of a logical mathematician. Not the madman from *The Eye of Eye*. I also found a short piece on Jan in a pre-World War I Polish newspaper, *Zgoda Małopolska*. From it, I learned that Cichy won several youth awards in mathematics. He was born in a small village of Wzrokienice in the Lesser Poland Voivodeship. After the 1939 invasion of Poland by the Nazis, the village was wiped out and its citizens butchered. And that he enjoyed nature hikes with his dog, Reki.

Years later, from other sources, I learned that Jan attended Jagiellonian University where he met Michał Nowak, and received a master's degree in mechanical engineering. At the age of 27, he immigrated to the United Kingdom with his parents and brother, Szymon. For reasons unknown—although it is heavily implied that Szymon was an opium addict, a fact that led to numerous fights—his brother emigrated to Spain, and never saw Jan or his parents again. While his parents settled in Showshill, Gloucestershire, Jan lived in London and, at first, worked for the Royal Railways, and, eventually, became employed as a patent clerk at the London Municipal Patent Bureau. He attended the University of London, but dropped out mere three credits away from gaining a degree in biology. Jan was fluent in Polish, English, German, and Russian.

He was known among his peers as eccentric, yet hard working. He was a self-taught inventor that held seventy-three patents before his disappearance. His mother describes him as an avid reader who really took to the works of Sigmund Freud. Between 1896-1901, he constructed, what he dubbed, the aero-craft, a hybrid of a boat and balloon. He hoped to be the first person to complete a latitudinal circumnavigation of the globe using the craft. He never achieved that goal.

He departed on his journey on February 4, 1901, the day of Queen Victoria's funeral. With Cichy's departure overshadowed by the Queen's burial, Jan is relegated to, what can only be called, the deep backwater of history. Did he complete his circumnavigation? No, he did not. There is a record of his departure via an article in *Gloucester Daily*, dated a day after his departure. For more details, please see the article's photocopy included before this introduction. However, somewhere west of Iceland something strange happened, and somehow—according to his account in *The Eye of Eyes*—Jan crash-landed on the Spanish coast. What happened next is described by him in this work, and clarified by Dr. Słowik in the afterword.

The Eye of Eyes is a strange little text, but before I get into that, a note on Adolf Hitler's fascination with the manuscript. Sometime between 1928-1939, Hitler must have read Daniel Kozuch's article on Jan Cichy in a German journal, *Schrecken des Geistes.* Mr. Kozuch came upon Jan's original manuscript after it had turned up in some dark corner of the University, and hoped to write his doctoral dissertation in it, but his academic adviser dismissed the idea. Instead, Mr. Kozuch wrote a short article that appeared in the German journal. In 1939, Hitler gave Alfred Rosenberg, who would become the Reich's head of the Ministry for the Occupied Eastern Territories (1941–1945), a direct order to deliver the manuscript to him upon the fall of Kraków. Hitler was obsessed with the city, and because the Nazis saw Kraków as an *urdeustche Stadt* (Ancient German City)—going as far as to create a pseudo-scientific institute to prove the city's German roots—everything within city limits was to be preserved, especially the libraries. Around this time, the manuscript disappeared from Jagiellonian University, and, thankfully, never reached Hitler. It was lost for several decades. Until 1976, when it was rediscovered in one of Rosenberg's undocumented properties that went up for sale, and promptly returned to the University. The legend goes that the man who delivered the manuscript hung himself outside the walls of the University's oldest part—the Collegium Maius, a few hours after dropping it off.

With some background knowledge on the author, I returned to the Library on Tuesday and, thankfully, the case filled the missing shelf space. The manuscript was mine for the remainder of the week. I read it several times. Why? Because it awakened some part of my own imagination. It provided me with a unique look at how Jan perceived culture, humanity, and his own role within it, and, in some ways, he echoed my own thoughts. It also provided me with an example of how madness looks from within the mind of a madman. Or perhaps, a sane Man, who had gone mad? Additionally, I was intrigued that the Polish used in the manuscript sounded modern. The tale itself reminded me of several weird horror books that I had read.

Jan's manuscript is a raving telling of how he ended up in a strange black plane not of this world. He swears that it happened. Then there is the titular Eye of Eyes. It is a chilling thing indeed. Three-fourth's way into the tale, Cichy returns to England via Spain. That is where his hallucinatory fantasy meets reality. This would be that section of the introduction where I would give a general outline of the story, but I do not think that is necessary. I think *The Eye of Eyes* speaks for itself. However, without spoiling too much, Cichy does end up somewhere in the Arabian Desert. I think such an end is poetics for a man who seems lost within his own internal wasteland.

After a week of meandering through Jan's mind, and having done very little real work, I forced myself to set the manuscript aside and dedicate my time to finishing my master's thesis, *On the Death of Originality*. Not until 2011 would *The Eye of Eyes* reenter my life. With the master's degree completed, I joined my friend Jeff Maslanik, on an epic journey through the Balkans, Romania, Bulgaria, Italy, and Malta. While taking a day to explore Belgrade on my own—after having already spent a week in the city—I ended up in an old bookshop, where I was lucky enough to snag an 1841 copy of Jean de La Fontaine's *Fables*.

It is in this book shop where I ran into the elderly beard man from that one Monday in 2009. Luck is a strange force indeed. With two years of exploring Europe and experiencing seedy and unusual things, I decided to approach this man and ask him about Cichy's manuscript. That is how I met this texts translator, Dr. Mirosław Słowik. We ended up in a café, then a bar. Like sand grains in an hourglass, the hours flew by. I learned that Dr. Słowik was in the process of translating *The Eye of Eyes* into English. We exchanged contact information and kept in touch. When he asked if I would be interested in writing an introduction to his translation, I agreed without hesitation. I invite everyone to read this wonderful work and, if possible, travel to Jagiellonian University and see the strange manuscript for themselves.

Adam Zmarzlinski
Kraków, 2019

Translator's Note

From that very first time in 1997 when I came across *Oko Oczu* in Jagiellonian University's Library, I knew that I would translate the piece from Polish into English. After several years of on and off translating, the work is finally finished. I chose to render the translation with as much chaotic poeticism as the original Polish manuscript in which it was written. Because the original manuscript is in, certain parts, raving and incomprehensible, while in others, the writing itself is illegible, I chose to include short notes throughout explaining these peculiarities. All the notes on such oddities are presented in-text in [brackets].

I chose to omit sections where Jan repeats what he had written. By that I mean that there are numerous pages in the original manuscript that are repeated up to four times in a rambling fashion. Paragraph formatting, as well as the eight-section breakdown, are my doing. The original manuscript is a flowing stream of consciousness that lacks in punctuation, capitalization, paragraph, or section breaks. Jan must have written the work in one exhausting and madness-induced night.

As. Mr. Zmarzlinski noted, the pages themselves, and the posted envelope in which they were sent, are swathed in strange symbols delicately penciled onto the pages. Meanwhile, the text itself is written in thick black ink, unless otherwise noted. Initially, I had hoped to include the symbols in this translation. However, for some strange reason every time we tried to scan or photograph the pages or ciphers, the result always came out smeared, as if someone slid their hand across the image. After several attempts, we gave up on including them.

Stubborn to have them included, I hired a local Krakówian artist, Arthur Głowacz, to recreate the symbols, but, as much as he tried, they came out childish in comparison to the originals. I mean no disrespect to Mr. Głowacz. He agreed that he did not do the originals justice. "There is something about them that excludes Man from the equation. It sounds silly, but they don't seem manmade to me," he told me over a beer. Due to these problems, the editors and I, chose not to include them. The only proper way to see and 'feel' the symbols is to travel to Jagiellonian University's Library and see them for yourself.

There are other strange eccentricities with the manuscript: every ninth page is written backwards and in reverse, meaning, for example, the continuation of page eight begins in the bottom right corner of page nine and is written in such a way that you need a mirror to read it. This happens only on every ninth page, and for the sake of readability (and sanity), I chose to translate and format those pages per normal reading standards. A bracketed note [backwards and reverse starts/ends] is added before and after each such sections. Page 99 is written entirely in Latin and is noted as such in this translation. Additionally, every sheet has Jan's fingerprint impression in the top right corner accompanied by the page number. This, in my opinion, and for reasons you will understand after reading this book, was to show the intended recipient that the manuscript was, in fact, written by the real Jan Cichy, and not some other version of him.

From a translator's perspective, this job had been a strange and exciting endeavor. It is a shame then that I am unable to coherently explain to the readers how odd and surreal it had been to translate this work. Often, and somehow unbeknownst to me, I would translate pages into German, or Russian or French. I would wake from some strange daydream, look back on the page, and be bewildered at the fact that none of what I had worked on for the past few hours were translated into English. *The Eye of Eyes* played tricks with my mind. I would translate a page or two in a café, and find myself in my flat without any recollection of having gotten there. I cannot explain it properly without sounding slightly ridiculous.

Another strange note when it comes to language: Jan never uses the word *umarł* or *umrzeć, odejść* or any of its variants, which in Polish are used when describing human death. It is a more civilized and humanized way of speaking of the subject matter. Instead, whenever discussing death, Jan uses the word *zdychać* and its variants, which refers to a brutal animalistic death, a death of a soulless creature. This is very unusual. One does not write like that in Polish. Furthermore, the phrase alters the meaning of death. It suggests that every 'character' who perishes in the text met an animalistic end. Unfortunately, the power of this phraseology will be lost to English-speaking readers.

Additionally: In between sections six and seven, Jan quotes Polish poet, Cyprian Kamil Norwid's "Ty Mnie Do Pieśni Pokornej Nie Wołaj" (Do Not Call Me to a Humble Hymn) poem in full. I kept the original and accompanied it with my own translation. All six quotes from Sigmund Freud's *The Interpretation of Dreams* were from the original German-language edition. I chose to usurp those quotes with the A. A. Brill English translation of the work. See footnotes for details.

This had been a 23-year-long project. I am glad that it is finally over. I hope that all who read this tale go on to tell others about it, and for those select few who get the chance to see the original manuscript in Kraków, I say, "Good luck trying to get it out of your mind." Whatever Jan Cichy saw, whether in a mad frenzy or not, the truth remains that none should see such horrors. Unfortunately, some already have, and, perhaps, some have seen worse.

Mirosław Słowik

Lisbon, 2021

AD 1901

My dearest friend,

Into the eyes of my own shadow I gazed, and saw nothing but a chasm of light. Rays burst forth as sharp as daggers piercing the very fabric of my conscience. Have you ever thought of what it means to exist? What it means to breath in and exhale? How expertly designed the process that keeps us alive is? In and out. Oxygen. Motion. Blood. Motion. Veins. Motion. Heart. Motion. Thoughts. Motion. Ad infinitum until we drop dead.

A drowning man, I have read, goes through a great many thoughts before his final one arrives, before the very last morsel of oxygen feeds his ravenous organs. I suppose, in general, a great deal of dying men think of a multitude of faces that they wish to apologize to. Faces they have failed or wronged or regretted. These personal multitudes—parents, friends, coworkers, lovers and the like—clawed at my mind as I took in, what I thought, was my last breath. Yet, their visit was brief. Quickly, they faded. Replaced by the lunacy beyond: a great black mare with blank eyes.

The mare of madness.

Its hoofs were bloody. Its legs caked with filth. It charged me. Although terrified, I stood defiant in this indescribable void, this expanse of nothingness.

I know that I'm not the only one who's seen this beast. There are many others. Perhaps, all dying men see it. The artist, Władysław Podkowiński,[1] saw it too and gave this horror shape in his 1894

1 A Polish painter and illustrator credited with bringing impressionism to Poland.

painting, *Frenzy of Exultations.* Upon the canvas, he expressed the dread, eroticism, and bliss that the mare stirs in a man. The right side of the canvas is solid black and out of this blackness emerges the great mare like a shadow out of time: eyes brimming with insanity, its tongue flipping wildly while foam disgorges from its lips. The horse rears into the left side of the canvas, its powerful front legs challenge the glow from the upper left, and hanging onto the horse's neck is a nude redhead. Her face is overwhelmed with ecstasy. She is free of the constraints of society, free from reason, free from anyone and everyone who has ever told her what to do, how to act or what to say. She is free. Period.

If you've not seen this painting, my friend, go to the National Museum[2] and see it. See it now. The mare upon that canvas freed me as much as it did the redhead. Its black mane, like demonic tentacles, embraced me in those abysmal depths that emerged from the Eye of Eyes. I cannot forget that Eye, that mighty thing which burst forth with undeniable truth. Everything we do and say every day is a lie.

You wake up only to wish you were asleep. You go to work against your own will, only so that your hands, your sweat, your time can make another man richer. And what do you get for this toil? An insignificant pittance to live off and endure in your small corner of squalor. These masses and their chickenfeed: they turn and buy a chain, some shackles, and with next week's pittance they buy gold paint so their fetters glimmer.

You do the work, day after day, like Sisyphus, but it's your neighbor's boulders that you struggle to roll up the hillside. The same neighbors who pack upon your back, like they would a beast of burden, heavy sacks of their own trifling tribulations. "Have I

---

2 Jan Cichy is referring to the *Muzeum Narodowe w Krakowie* (National Museum in Kraków) where many of Władysław Podkowiński's works are displayed.

told you of my job?" "Well, Julia is getting married to…" "I don't know what to do about…" And they sigh with self-pity. And what of that great lie, of comradery? Instead of coworkers, of brothers and sisters in flesh, helping and aiding one another, we become vermin like starving rats biting and probing each other inside a sweltering furnace, so that the treacherous ones among us can get up top while the rest burns in inferno and wail.

You come home from that grind, from commands of lesser men, from jumping between one hoop then another, and now you're faced with all the trifles of home: keep your wife happy, raise your kids into decency, clean the living room, keep it nice, cut the grass, so that one day you can resell it and die elsewhere. And the family. They bend you into a twisted version of yourself, "Why didn't you do this?" "Why didn't you marry her?" "Why not work for so and so?" And with every question there is another bag of stones placed upon your back so that each step is heavier and slower than the one that preceded it.

And finally, after all the mazes he's ran through and bruises he's gained, a man goes and works on something he enjoys. In that solace, he realizes that there is so little time to accomplish one's own plans because first he must realize the plans of others: employers, mothers, fathers, friends, children. Throughout this labyrinth of life, parasites in human skins prey upon you: the landlord, the tax collector, the priest, the policeman, the municipal master, and so on. All of them with their hand out, and all of them promising and all of them lying. And all that's left is a smaller pittance with less time and then you die. Sometimes you have to die. Sometimes that's all there is left to do.

You're lowered into the dirt to be eaten by worms and maggots unless you're a coward. Then you're cremated and the dark ash to which people attached a proper name, with proper values, is placed into a chamber pot and thrown out, like rubbish, into the pastures, the sea, from mountain tops, so that a memory of you can be evoked only by the wind that carried your smithereens along.

What I just described to you, my friend, is the madness, the great lie, that we all call normal or rational or proper. The Eye of Eyes, the mare, it showed me, freed me of this 'reason' and birthed several more *I*s into this world. I keep on invading myself, and I keep on strangling them as they try to take me. I…I…

[Several illegible paragraphs.]

It doesn't matter, the Legion is coming. Wars and bloodshed and tears and laughter. It will all be here soon. There will be a great deal of hilarity and then a deafening silence. I know, I've seen it. It coursed through me, through my being, my metaphysical self. I pray to the God Almighty that he releases me of these images and sensation: I see them everywhere. Everywhere. If I could only go back to that moment in time, I would have never left. Never! I would have indulged in normalcy. I would have bathed in what is expected of me. I would have been an obedient fellow who would have accepted his life as is as all the countless generations before me had. But 'would haves' are simply nostalgic regrets, and for those I have no more space, no more time. All is madness. All is right.

I

FOR YEARS, I'VE studied Jean-François de Rozier, Francois d'Arlanders and Montgolfier's balloon designs.[3] I've read all the da Vinci manuscripts, and much of the meteorological works by Aristotle, Theophrastus, Al-Dinawari, Alhazea, Bacon, Beaufort, Fahrenheit, Celsius, Pascal and all the rest.[4] I dedicated thousands of hours between all the nonsensical clerical work at the patent office to build the first ever aero-craft. Half balloon, half ship. Small in size, but steerable and capable of self-propulsion. Five years it took me, but I did it. I did it. It was the only thing that I truly cared about. Only thing I wanted to finish.

I thought of including all the technical data in this letter. At first, to have a testament of the data itself, of the measurements and charters and ideas, flat on paper. I thought of how important it would be to have it here as proof that I was able to imagine and build it all before anyone else did. I thought, perhaps, that you'd enjoy looking over the schematics and blueprints, my friend, but I decided against it. Not out of fear or judgment or some other human emotion, but simply out of the data's insignificance when compared to God's blueprints. Once the Eye showed me the truth, I realized that all this science that I've worked on for so long was

3 French aviation pioneers.

4 Philosophers and science pioneers.

like that of a petty child playing in a sandbox. None of the work amounted to anything else but a temporary sand structure whose destiny was to be washed away by the waves of the infinite sea of time.

In early 1901, the aero-craft was ready. I tested it a few times, flying over the trees at my parent's farm in Snowshill, Gloucestershire. As I saw deficiencies with the rudder, gas flow or balloon swelling, I tuned the various mechanics. It was time-consuming, detail-oriented work, not of the bureaucratic type, but of the technical one. Meaning that a few small mistakes now, could become major problems as I flew over the Pacific or the poles. The pressure valves were uncooperative at first but… Why do I write all this? I'm not sure. It's all just unnecessary wiring. Whatever human part of me that remains seeks acknowledgement for the work I once did. It's that human desire for commendation. A melancholy need for a pat on the back.

I was ready to take off on February 2nd. I was going to do the impossible, my friend, I was going to take my aero-craft and be the first person to latitudely circumnavigate the world. Months of preparations: rechecking the balloon daily, polishing the hull and inspecting for any punctures or cracks. I carefully packed the storage alcoves with supplies. A little engine I built made the steering of the craft much easier, but it ate up petrol, so I had to place the petrol barrels around the hull proportionality to the weight of the whole to keep the craft balanced. Gas canisters, too, had to be taken into consideration. The craft had to fly. The balloon had to keep the whole sky-locked. All that time in preparation, all that stress. All a distant memory.

My dear mother would often come into the barn and silently watch as I obsessed over the details. She said very little. She was concerned, I knew. One does get worried when they see someone they love consumed by one thing or another. They see the humanity drain out of them and become replaced by thing-lust, by a selfish desire to become some*thing* other than what we are. The 20th century will be just that: a constant thing-lust, a process of dehumanization and becoming more thing-like, more obedient and disgusted with freedom. Freedom will become associated with choice, and choice will become shunned, because to choose is to have a potential at suffering, and in a mechanical future there is no room for pain, only pleasure.

On January 21, I took a train from Gloucester to London. I took a week off from my clerical work at the patent office and returned to my small flat in Islington Borough to organize the flat and ready myself for two meeting that I had scheduled the following day. The first with Prof. William Golder of Imperial College, London, the other with Mr. Friedmore Lancaster Jr. of the *Times.* Both meetings concerned my journey and, I hoped, were stepping stones in the promotion of my adventure.

Earlier in the week, I met with Mr. Homer Essayd at the *Gloucester Daily* and discussed the expedition. Mr. Essayd noted that he'd write up a small piece for the *Daily* on February 1st, to make the local readership aware of the take off.[5] It was a delightful interview, Mr. Essayd was genuinely interested in my venture. Asking about how I'd handle the freezing temperatures of the poles, the desperate loneliness of open sea, and what I'd eat while out there in the wilds, he demonstrated the inquisitiveness of an explorer. It was refreshing to speak with a man so keen on learning about others, but in retrospect, it was my vanity that sat satisfied with the interview. Again, the human need for acknowledgment overpowered my reason. Nonetheless, it was a truly exciting time for me.

Prof. Golder awaited me in his office and we spoke of all the little patents I had lined up to file after my journey. I recall little

---

5 A reprint of the article is available at the beginning of this book. The article was published one day after Jan's departure on February 5, 1901.

of our conversation as Prof. Golder came off as a much duller man than the one I'd written to. Biophysics was his specialization. Unfortunately, if there lived any imagination in the man, it was squeezed out of him by the academy long ago. We mostly discussed hydration and biological systems theory but all in the context of the classroom. Every experiment he spoke of was of the safe variety that appeased the literature and progressed nothing beyond his career. I did not come to this man for inquiry into theory A, B or C. I wanted to explore a great mind, I explored a mediocre one at best. I conversed with a sophist on what I needed to discuss with a philosopher.

The conversation frustrated me, so I asked him directly, "What do you think the will of invention is in comparison to the will of academia?" He seemed to have been confused by the question, as he answered that the will of invention is the will of academia. I couldn't help myself and laughed at his cowardice. "You're telling me academia wishes for innovation?"

"Well, of course. Science must be our guide and we must take it as the compass to how the world works. Only science can lead us to progress."

"You sound like a man who speaks of science in similar terms to an 11th century monk who spoke of the Church and its Pontiff as 'our only way toward progress.' Don't get me wrong, sir, science should be followed, but it shouldn't be the be all, end all solution. Science is, in its very essence, just another Tower of Babel."

He was outraged by my proposition. I continued, "Academia's only role is to uphold the status quo and milk as much gold coin from the taxpayer's udder as it can. It demonizes anything new and clings to the theories of its day. It shuts down novel ideas unless they can bring it coin or recognition. And even then, it only uses those ideas as a tool that once worn can be disposed of. Everything else it sees as chaff in the wind."

I recall leaving his office angry. The very fact that this man, who sits in such a prominent position, this man who had no experience beyond the university setting, is seen as a paragon of his craft, disgusted me. It proved to me that what I've contemplated for a long time: that common men know not the intellectual swindling that the priest, the scholar, and the banker wield. The snake oil salesman has moved out from the rattlesnake infested wilderness and into the bureaucracy of the modern world. Instead of selling miracle ointments, he sells intellectual gobbledygook and says, 'This is an idea! This will make your life better!' What a farce.

This prominent academic applied theory to everything and to such an extent that he'd never get anything done practically. In many ways, he reminded me of several of the bureaucrats with whom I worked with at the patent office. There was a divide between the reality in their head and the tangibility outside of it. The reality outside carried no details of the one they promoted. And what they promoted they validated with unending tongue flapping. They spent no sweat, no grind, no will to create it. Hypocrisy was their reality. It's a shame, of course, that such people are in charge of the masses, such empty husks with no creativity, imagination or daring. These armchair adventurers will accomplish nothing and yet they are always the first to cast doubt and ill word against those who wish to truly change the world, or better yet challenge themselves.

These sad souls reminded me very much of what Sigmund Freud wrote in his new volume, *The Interpretation of Dreams*, which I was reading at the time. Freud mentioned that "the dream often reveals to us what we do not wish to admit to ourselves, and that we therefore unjustly condemn it as a liar and deceiver."[6] The denial these men of trivial creativities are able to conjure are impressive.

---

6 Instead of translating Freud from its original German, the translator will be using A. A. Brill's translation of the text. Hereafter: Freud, Sigmund. *The Interpretation of Dreams*. Translated by A. A. Brill. New York: Barnes & Noble Classics, 2005. 68.

They see before them reality, or maybe even the potential of reality, and reject it outright for some theory that holds no anchor in the truth but floats on high like a dandelion puff. A soft lie will carry them further than the hard truth. Perhaps, that is what they cling to it so as not to be on intimate terms with a noose.

What else can I write, my friend? The meeting with the professor was a complete waste of time. But, I was not defeated, no! I still had ahead of me an interview with the newspaperman from the *Times*. I floated about on high optimism. Mr. Friedmore Lancaster Jr., was an honorable and intelligent sort. Even though he was aware of my employment, he asked about my clerical work out of politeness. He surprised me when mentioning my small 1899 art exhibit at Quarter Hall. He even had one of my announcement pamphlets. "Your landscapes are very pleasant," he motioned to a postcard print of one of my works. I was quite embarrassed by his having of such a plethora of information on my person. He was aware of my studying at Jagiellonian University, my emigration to the Kingdom, and even the family's land dispute with my younger brother, who, as you know, fled to Spain, some years ago. Mr. Lancaster was a true journalist.

Our conversation flowed pleasantly and indeed Mr. Lancaster was an expert on how to formulate an interesting article. He hoped to write about my fleeing of Galicia with the family and how it led to my fleeing of conventional ideas of what can and cannot be done with modern science and engineering. Once I explained to him how my aero-craft worked, he was quick to ask about its social and civilizational potential. "Surely, there is something there for a betterment of mankind," he suggested. I made sure to stress that once the craft was tested via my circumnavigation, I had a great many patents that I wished to file. "Indeed, I think a fully functioning flying machine will be a great benefit to the world," I told him. "But it must be a tested benefit, not a theoretical one." That must have impressed him, as he jotted it down in his notebook.

"Perhaps, I should focus the article on the meteorological and inventor aspect of your person, Mr. Cichy," he told me. "I understand you studied engineering at university, but that before joining the patent office, you volunteered at the UK's branch of the International Meteorological Organization?"

I agreed at first and explained my amateur interests in meteorology, specifically the works of Léon Teisserenc de Bort, Max Margules, Svante Arrhenius and the like.[7] This too he noted in his notebook. I suggested that, perhaps, it is wiser to present a creative and daring side to a man when writing of such adventurous. "The public prefers pomp over intellectuality," I told him. "It gives the public more confidence in the adventure while providing the more elite thinkers among them to describe the merits of such and such a fellow's ability to complete their venture. It keeps people talking, is what I suggest."

He nodded.

"Please do not mention anything about my artistic endeavors," I said spontaneously. He seemed to understand. An artist-adventurer is not something the people support. They perceive artist-adventurers as worthless lazy bodies. An artist is a dreamer, and a dreamer gets more ridicule than he does funds. My hopes were that after the expedition, and patenting of my aero-craft and its various components, I would see some investment from interested industrialists. It was a dream of course. As you will read, the journey did not end in my favor. Or perhaps it did.

[Jan repeats "Or perhaps it did," 34 times in various languages and fonts.]

As I spoke of the finer details of the craft, I believe it was the ability to steer the balloon using a small petrol engine I devised, a man ran into the café and screamed, "The Queen Victoria is dead!" and ran off. That was January 22.

7 French, Austrian, and Swedish (respectively) scientists and meteorological pioneers.

Mr. Lancaster became visibly excited. "Good day, sir," he said, picked up his quill and notebook, and ran off in pursuit of the story. The whole city was abuzz about the death of the Queen. It sickened me to my very core. When a normal man dies, he gets no applause or tears from the public, but when this ruthless beast of the royal did, all of Britain wept. I did not cry for king August Poniatowski, nor for Napoleon III, I did not cry for the Queen.[8]

After my expedition, when I returned to London, I found out that Mr. Lancaster never wrote that piece for the *Times* and perhaps that is exactly what needed to happen. Perhaps, beside myself, and soon you, no one should be aware of my failure. No one will know.

With the city ablaze with the news of the dead queen, I ended up doing the only reasonable thing and wandered the streets for a couple of hours. I could have gone to my flat and rested, but to see pigs cry over the death of the butcher was a much more interesting proposition. Everyone had some tale they mildly recalled about how once they saw the Queen. "I saw her leave the Palace once, I did," said some bearded street preacher. "She was in a regal coach of gold. Oh, our beautiful Queen! Heaven bound she is." "She was a golden child she was," a woman told a group of lads. "I heard she had the Lord's cross with her at all time. Best act right and go pray for her soul." The lunacy that sprouted from the death of this one woman, whom clearly none of them knew anything about, was both frightening and fascinating. The madness of crowds is at its finest when ignorance administers the reigns. Having had enough of this pointlessness, I headed over to King's Cross and returned to Gloucester.

I needed the silence, so Fortune granted me an empty cabin. For the past two days, my world has been in a turmoil. Anxiety and fear about the expedition fueled me. The passing country and

8 Respectively: the last king of Poland, and the first president of France.

the train's charging forward through the landscape calmed me a bit more than it should have. Movement, I think, of any sorts, was my sedative.

As I recounted all the things that still needed to be done, a man entered the cabin and sat across from me. I stared outside, watching the overcast countryside, when a strange feeling of being watched assailed me. I glanced at my cabin companion. He was a normal looking man in a brown suit. Nothing about him seemed abnormal. Then I focused on his eyes. One of them was without a pupil. Instead a serpent, perhaps, the ouroboros, coiled itself about.

"The Eye frightens everyone," the man said. "It is unusual. It is not something you can gaze into. Not a glimmer of the soul of Man can be found inside it. It's simply there: a serpent on a white background."

"Beg my pardon, but did you lose it in a war?"

The man smiled and stared at me in silence.

[Backwards and reverse starts.]

"The Dogū are small humanoid figures made during the late Jōmon period of pre-historic Japan," he began. "These figurines are beautifully decorated with small feet, large shoulders and immense eyes that sit atop their strange oblong head. Archeologists and treasure hunters have no idea what they are for, they have no context for their eyes. Some say they are human effigies, some that they are representations of the gods. Others, yet note, that illnesses and ill will could be transferred into them and the statues then destroyed in a ceremony."

"I've seen them in the British Museum," I told him, as if that had anything to do with what he was saying.

He ignored me and continued, "Their goggle-like eyes have been noted to resemble that of some versions of a diving suit. Curious theories. Some interesting to discuss for the sake of conversation. All of them wrong. The Eyes of the Dogū are a dedication to the Eye of Eyes. They are a tangible wish. A wish that Man, too, had eyes that can see beyond time and space, beyond this finite reality. The Eye has entered the Earth Dream a few times in the past. Once in Hokkaido, currently Northern Japan, where it gifted Man fire. It moved southward to Niigata where it grew bored and moved on. A little shrine sits on Mount Myōkō to celebrate the departure. When it appeared in the past, it did so to teach. Unfortunately, its lessons are often lost on mortal minds. Men are too brittle for truth. Too ego-centric for selfless wisdom."

"That is an interesting tale," I told the stranger who, frankly, began to annoy me.

"Tale. Yes," he said and smiled subtly.

I returned to the passing countryside. The stranger switched seats and sat beside me. A strange scent of overwhelming sweetness of a candy shop combined with rancid meat filled my nostrils.

"You know, Mr. Cichy," the man began. "There hides within each of us a want, a need really, for the weight that we carry to be carried by another version of us. Often, I've spoken to folks who say, 'I wish there were two of me, one to do the work and one to do the resting."

I scooted away from the man and sat as close to the window as possible. He continued, "The masses dream of having duplicate slaves of themselves. The dream of identical servants, but only for all the work, chores, and dull acts, but for none of the pleasantries, for none of the deliciousness of life. Duplicate dreamers abound. Why do you think that is?"

"I don't know, sir, and to be honest, it is none of my concern. I am not one of these duplicate dreamers, as you call them."

[Backwards and reverse ends.]

"A short story I once read, Mr. Cichy," he repeated my name, even though I did not introduce myself, "titled *The Many Hands of Mine* by some no-name author presented me with an answer. In it, the story that is, a workman, let's call him Frank, wakes up one morning after a particularly hard day's work and decides not to go into the smelting mill. He laments, 'I've had enough. Cramped muscles, aching back, hazy eyes, charred hands. I'd do anything for someone else to do the work for me.' Suddenly, a knock sounds on Frank's door and a little fella, let's call him Apollyon, appears and, with great wit and delightful verses, proposes to split Frank into two selves: one to work and one to stay home to do as he wishes. No catch at all. 'No catch, huh?' Frank confirms and Apollyon swears on his mother's grave, 'No catch.' Frank agrees to the deal. *Poof* and two Franks stand in the living room. One goes to work while the other decides to get himself some beer and lay out in the backyard.

"All is well, until the hero's wife, Francine, comes home from her mother's and scolds our hero. 'Why aren't you at work, you bum?' she hollers, but our hero is ready with a lie: 'I have the day off because the mill is shut down for some maintenance.' 'Perfect,' she replies. 'You can do some work around the house.' And she writes up a whole list of chores for poor Frank to do, then jollies off to her sister's. But this poor fella just wants to rest. Isn't that what every man really wants to do: catch a moment of respite from the demands of others?

"Again, Apollyon arrives and asks Frank if he wishes for, yet another, double. 'Yes, yes!' the chap replies. *Poof.* Another Frank to do the chores. As is the trope with these tales, this process goes on for a few more examples: the hero's uncle dies and his family needs to be taken care of, his mother falls ill and someone needs to help her out, the children are acting up so there needs to be a father to discipline them, and so on. Well eventually there are nine Franks.

"Now that Frank's life is in order and he does nothing but drink—because the other Franks are living his life—Apollyon appears once more and gives our hero an ultimatum: if he want this easy life to continue, he must agree to sign a little contract that if he is ever dissatisfied with his current state of affairs all the Franks will return to being one and their responsibilities will become his again. 'I'm not signing my soul away, am I?' a drunk Frank asks. 'Not unless you want to, but that is a different form,' Apollyon jokes. Weeks go by and all goes well. Until one day, an outraged mob appears at the pub and wants Frank's head on a pike. 'For what?' Frank asks. 'I've been here drinking.' Well the mob lists a flurry of reasons: for burning down a shop, for a murder of a pawnshop broker, for theft, owing money to a great deal of bankers, sleeping with a great deal of married women, and, of course, his wife is there to ask for divorce.

"As you could imagine, Frank is quite confused but quickly realizes that perhaps his doubles acted upon their own impulses after they completed their chores. Each person dwells in their own desires and weaknesses, so why wouldn't one's doubles? There and then, Frank decides it is time to go back to being responsible for one's choices. *Poof.* Old Franky finds himself in prison, with one arm and one leg and a date with the noose set for the morning. He screams and he protests. All in vain, of course. Apollyon appears one final time and tells our hero that he must pay for his sloth and all the sins of all the versions of him that existed and exist.

"The tale ends with a great little monologue about how there are as many versions of us as there are people who have met us and for each interpretation of us there is a sin. Since there were nine Franks, his sins were multiplied ninefold. In the morning, Frank is hung. The end."

"That is quite a melancholy story," I said.

"Melancholy stories are eulogies to our sins, and proclamations of future ones," the man replied with a smile, stood up and, closing the door behind him, exited the cabin. Where he sat there remained a small curved misshapen piece of what looked like glass. It shined with a dark glimmer. I picked it up. A warmth spread up my fingers, until it grew infernally hot. I let go of the fragment and it slid down into my palm. A thousand skeletal faces appeared in the glass. As if it were a drop of water, my palm absorbed it. A painful heat surged up my arm, through the neck, and into my head where it seared my mind like a scorching brand.

The next thing I knew, the conductor shook me into wakefulness.

"We've arrived, sir," he said. "We're in Gloucester." I checked my palm. It looked as normal as ever but I felt some*thing* pulsate within the flesh. I must have left after that, perhaps giving the conductor a scare. I felt like a wraith gliding through the world. Everything lay covered in cobwebs and mist. I remember little of how I returned to my parent's farm. I'm sure I must have taken a cab back, but my memory is vague at best.

I woke up a day later just as the sun rose.

"You feeling well?" my father asked as I entered the kitchen.

I nodded.

"You slept yesterday away," he said handing me a mug of tea. I thanked him and we sat drinking in silence. Steam rose from the mug and disappeared into nothingness as it neared the ceiling. My father sighed. He did that when something bothered him.

"What is it?" I asked. Sipping his tea, he stared at me for a moment.

"Why did you become an office clerk?" he asked. "You have a Master's degree in engineering."

"I told you," I began, alluding to the dozens of similar conversations I had with him in the past, "the English, like the Americans, don't accept degrees from other countries. Sure, they talk of acceptance and merit, but think of immigrants as third class citizens. Most of the time, we're just parasites to them. Scapegoats, of course. They only hired me because I know the system and can notice design similarities without searching through hundreds of volumes of patent tomes."

"Bureaucratic thugs," my father said. "Armies of worthless bureaucrats sitting on their asses adding noting to the world but flaming hoops for normal people to jump through."

I nodded. He wasn't wrong. Most office work is dull, mundane, and as close to mental torture as can be. These office crustaceans work an hour or two out of the day, the rest they spend gossiping or reading papers. The only thing they add to the world is another job title.

"I never wanted you to become a bureaucrat," he said wiping his mustache. "Scum of the world, be it in Poland, Austro-Hungry or here. They follow their codes and rules, no exceptions, no humanity in their cold eyes, always spewing forth clerical jargon to confuse the common man. Where is the dignity in such work? Where is the honor?"

We sat silently.

"They're thieves you know," he began. "Working off the taxes of the laborer, the builder, the farmer. These Kings and Queens and nobles aren't any better. They never pay in blood. When Napoleon rolled through Europe the people had to pay in fear and fire. They fed the earth their blood to make it fertile." He paused to sigh. "All those farms and fields overgrown with wheat, trodden by cattle that feed on the grass nourished by seas-worth of blood, and come another war, it will happen again."

"There was an article in the paper last week. They found 300 bodies of German and French soldiers near Jena. Some still held their muskets," I said. My father's eyes grew teary.

"You should have become a pharmacist not a parasite," my father said. It broke me inside to hear this. He said nothing about my work on the aero-craft. I know he meant well. He did. The memories of occupied Poland under Austro-Hungarian control made him bitter. He wanted a free Poland with free Poles. Instead his compatriots had to flee their homeland or become slaves to brutal masters: Prussians, Russians, or the Habsburgs.

"Feel these hands," he told me, motioning his palm toward mine. I did. They were rough and felt like dry bark. Thick veins flowed across the top his hairy hands. There was a plethora of scars that ran along his fingers and palm.

"From years of farm work," he said. "From the time in the army," he pointed to a nasty scar that began at the pinky and ran along the side of his hand. "A bayonet went through. They say the eyes are the windows to the soul, but hands are the windows to one's past."

He grabbed my hand. "These are soft. Plump. I run my fingers along and I feel gentleness and a lack of struggle. Look," he showed me my own hand. "No callous spots, no scars, no blemishes, only fresh flesh. I don't envy you these hands. Your mother and I worked hard so that you wouldn't have the hands of a laborer."

He walked over to the sink and washed his tea mug. "I hoped for you to be pharmacist. It's a steady job. People will continue to be sick. Costumers are plentiful. But with bureaucrats…" He shook his head. "I hope that balloon thing you've got in there is worth the toil."

"It is," I said. "It's the only thing I feel right about." He surveyed me one last time, put on his jacket and rain boots, and went out to the pens to let the sheep out to pasture.

My parents sold everything they owned in Poland to come to Britain. They settled outside of Gloucester, in the sleepy village of Snowshill, bought a farm, some sheep, and made their living selling wool and making cheese. Business was good, the money was good, and for the first time in a long time, they weren't hounded by Polish bureaucrats looking for a bribe. Those were the rules of Eastern Europe: need to put up a shed, pay a bribe, then you'll get a permit; need a doctor to see you, pay a bribe, then you'll die in a bed, not in the hallway; need to sell something, pay a bribe for the stamp of approval, then you're free to do what you want with what *you* own. It's not Eastern Europe without bribes. Nevertheless, it's not much different from the West. Here they call bribes taxes. 'You gotta do your duty for the sake of the nation and the crown,' bootlickers often say. At least in the East you know that you're getting something jammed up your bum, in the West they are blissfully ignorant of it. They feel it, sure, but they think it's just a natural part of civilization: Adam Smith's invisible fist up the citizen's hind.

I thought about what my father said then dressed and went out to the back barn to prepare the aero-craft. As I crossed the pasture, I saw something white slither about in the frigid fog. I walked into the misty depths, which often rolled through from the Atlantic, to witness a thick white serpent slink between the grass. I followed it until it had disappeared into a mole mound. I peered into the darkness of the earth. A scent of sour meat with hints of candy shop sweetness permeated my nostrils. A hollow sound, like metal scraping against stone, echoed from far off. I stared into the fog, and felt something staring back. My hands perspired and my heart beat intensified. I can't explain it, but something watched me from within the miasma.

After composing myself, I went to the barn and prepared the craft for the morning's full-cargo launch. I had enough helium, petrol, and propane. I fitted a small oil drum at the stern for the handling of the directional turbine and packed enough canned and pickled food to last me eight weeks, which would be enough time to reach Alaska, where I'd resupply the craft.

My biggest worry lay in the flight path over the Pacific Ocean. There is nothing between Alaska and Antarctica but water and some minor island nations. To be lucky enough to find and land on any one of these islands was a stretch. I was well versed in the craft's operational capabilities but my navigational skills were not as well-honed as I'd wish. All the meteorological equipment in the craft was calibrated. I had plenty of warm clothes to get me across the Arctic and Antarctica circles. These, too, were great challenges in their own right because of the freezing cold and potential blizzards. However, I was confident in the aero-craft's durability at high altitudes, even above-cloud heights. I believe the human body cannot breathe and maintain itself seven kilometers above ground. Thus, in times of crisis, such as a storm or blizzard, it was vital for me to know when to make the aero-craft go above the clouds and when to bring it down. I took in the Earth's spin as well. My calculations would have to be adjusted daily, even hourly, depending on wind drag. Overall, I was ready.

After a day's worth of work, I felt it was time for a much-needed rest.

As I returned to the house, my father herded the sheep back into the pens. I looked at my hands, at where that piece of glass melted into my palm. I ran my finger along its soft flesh. My father was right. These were the hands of a man who had never really worked through hardship. The older I get, the more it seems to me that wisdom is not about what you know, but about knowing what it is that you don't know and acting accordingly regardless of that fact. I went up to my room, washed up, and decided to go to bed without a meal. I hoped fasting would keep my mind clear 'till the morning, but before I settled into sleep, my mother came in with a plate of ground beef patties, salted potatoes, and some pickled vegetables.

"How you feeling?" she asked.

"Unsure," I replied.

She observed me and placed the plate on my writing desk. "Eat," she said and I did. She sat down on my bed and spoke while I ate. She often did this. It gave her a chance to say her piece without interruption.

"I don't want you to fly off," she began. "It's unnatural to be up there were God is. I know that the assessment flights went well. I don't care. All those summer tests flights, they chilled me to the bone. This whole flying idea…of being up there in the nothingness, it's dangerous. You shouldn't be playing adventurer while men your age are getting married and moving up the career ladder at work."

There was a chasm of silence between us. Only the sound of

utensils moving and food being chewed resonated throughout the space.

"What do you think will come of this, Jan? You go up there and fly across the sea, nothing but water, nothing but air. I've prayed to Saint Christopher[9] to keep you under his protection, but out there in that frozen waste, there are no saints, only godlessness and the cold hand of Dante's Satan." She walked up to the table and placed down a thin golden necklace with a Saint Christopher medallion attached to it. "Please take this and keep it on you at all times."

"Will do," I said.

"I don't approve of any of this," she continued. "I'd rather you fly that thing around Snowshill than out there into the boundless depths. You must start thinking of us, too. Your father and I are getting older. A time will come when he won't be able to tend to the sheep. We'll need someone to help us out around the farm. Your brother chose to flee to Spain. He chose to leave us behind. And when the time comes, you'll need someone to help you, too. You'll need a wife. Meanwhile, you're taking months off from work, spending money on all sorts of gadgets, playing inventor. Life is short, Jan. You'll have to make do with your choices. Especially when they are folly and childish stubbornness and—"

"That's enough," I cut in. "I understand that you're worried about me, but look at what you and father are: you're farmers. Your whole life's been toil. I don't want that for myself, which doesn't mean that I don't understand the worth of hard work. I go into the office day in and day out and all I gain from it is some pittance to feed and house myself with. What kind of existence is that?"

"That is life, Jan."

"Perhaps," I paused. "I could be like everyone else: work,

9 Patron saint of travelers.

spend my time in the pubs, go to bed only to wake up and do it all over again: bed, work, pub, ad infinitum."

"But if you had yourself a good woman—"

"And be like you and father? You spend days not talking to one another. I'm not naïve enough to think that I'll fall in love and, *bam!* its happily ever after. I've seen those old couples. Five, ten, fifteen years in, and it sets in: relationship fatigue. It doesn't take long before people realize that they've made a mistake. People can talk with each other for only so long before the conversations dry up. I'm not made for mindless office work or routine marriages. Such things are fine for those who seek them. But how long will it be of the repetitive tedium before I tie a noose, find a sturdy beam, and call it quits?"

"And how do you plan to feed yourself, Jan? Ideas don't put food on the table."

"I built a damn flying machine. I did that. You know anyone else who has done that? People make sacrifices for their children, for their careers, well, I sacrificed for that thing in the barn. It's demoralizing that you lecture me on what I should do, but give me no praise for what I've already achieved."

My mother sighed. "Don't forget this," she tapped her finger at the Saint Christopher medallion then left the room. I finished my meal in silence. Before washing up the plate downstairs, I stared out the window, watching the rolling clouds that accompanied the setting sun, for a while. People make life more complicated than it really is. Their constant need for interjecting in the lives of other makes them prisoner to their own self-admiration.

In the morning, I flight tested the aero-craft with all its cargo. The test went better than I anticipated. The elevation altimeter, pressure barometer, and steering module worked without fail. A sense of joy that I haven't felt in a long time washed over me.

[What follows is four pages of 'joy, happiness, ecstasy,' and synonyms of these terms written in various languages and handwritings. At the bottom right-hand corner of each page, sits some sort of rodent paw print pressed into the paper in a luminescent ink. The edges of each page are decorated with counter-clockwise spirals and the numbers 1, 7, 10, 13, 19, 23, 33, 49, 70, 79, 86, 88, 94, 96 and 100 in various colored inks.]

I spent the next few days charting my course and correcting trajectory equations. The days passed in concentration and silence. My mother and father barely spoke to me. Much of my time was spent in the barn, checking and rechecking the aero-craft and its various components. I kept on reminding myself that everything was fine. Yet, something in the back of my mind, some nagging pessimism, disagreed.

Paradoxical thinking is a curse. It can make a man indecisive and yoked to his own opinion. I often thought of and agreed with two opposing ideas at the university. It made written exams that much harder to complete. When I began my tenure at the patent office, I despised the work, but saw how important patenting good ideas could be. To create without financial gain is a curse of every great mind. Most brilliant men die in poverty. It's only after they die that their work is praised, then it's someone else who profits off their labor. All of life seems to be that way: contradiction and theft. How often did I contradicting myself? How often did I take the style or idea of another? Every piece of art, every design and sketch, I've ever produced blares 'Impostor!' to the world. All the chest-fulls of painted parchments and canvas prints, all the time invested in their creation, and to what end?

When I die all of it will be forgotten, tossed into a rubbish bin to decompose in a heap of trash on the outskirts of this or that city. And what do I get from creating, anyway? Is it a release of some depths that lie bottled up within? Or a need for an audience, a need of approval from my fellow vermin? I don't know. I think no creature really knows. All these musicians, writers, painters—creators—give differing reasons for why they do what they do. Most explanations are fabricated and selfish. Simple tropes for simple masses. A few of them are honest and thought-provoking, but those are a rare sight, like blooming flowers atop mountain caps.

You said it best a long time ago, my friend. It was around the time when you just finished your doctoral dissertation: "I did this thing to do it and now that it is done, it's as if there was no need to do it in the first place." Ain't that the truth? We do this or that, yet at the end of the day, we sit still in our living room and waste away. Some gossip with friends, others read a book with brandy in hand, others count their coffers (or potential coffers), others still lay in bed and weep while a phonograph plays Wagner or Chopin or whomever. No matter the events of the day, they all go to sleep the same, wake up the same, and, in the end, succumb to regret the same.

But when they're awake, when they're in polite company among the masses, they all praise this great author, that great ruler, whomever it might be that is the talk of the town that day. Cliché and worthless lip service to men and women who have no real bearing or influence over their lives. Odysseus turned to the swineherd, Eumaeus, for help upon his return to Ithaca, not to the bards, the statesmen, the prodigious philosophers. He went to where toil and strength lay. That is the reason that I will always listen to my parent's advice, even though I may not agree with it. There is more sage wisdom in the speeches of swineherds than scholars. Yet, it is the professor of engineering who's praised, not the engineer. The professor of art over the artist. The professor of philosophy over the philosopher.

Vert little of who we are and what we really think leaves our lips and fingers. So much babble, I've heard, so much nonsense, about what this man or that fellow had read in today's paper. Almost never do I hear what they think of what it is they read. Almost always they quote me some reporter or expert, some other person that isn't them. People's opinions are quotes. People's craniums echo chambers. This inability to speak freely, to speak at all, makes madmen out of them. If only wise men could speak and the crowds listen, not even agree or disagree, but just to give the words consideration, perhaps, this world would be a better one. Instead, senseless men talk of idle things to idle ends. Then, at death's door, they wonder why they haven't achieved anything. Meanwhile, Fate blares in their ear, "It's because you followed the rules of polite society, you fools!" The comedy of tragedy, my friend!

The Eye had shown me the truth. It had graced me with reality. Emptiness rules people. Sometimes, rarely, real significance emerges from one of them and for that they are mocked and besmirched by lesser wits. And what praise comes their way comes as misunderstanding. I know of no men as misunderstood, and misinterpreted, as Jesus Christ and Athens's own, Socrates. These are men of timeless ideas, ideas that do not define one age, but all of them. Today's academicians laugh at these giants. While Jesus and Socrates sit atop sky-bound peaks, scholars mock them from their molehills. Crowds cheer the ideas of pigmies and, unfortunately, when I launched my aero-craft on February 4th, the world cheered for one such pigmy, Queen Victoria.

Everything was ready but no one came. The fields of Snowshill watched the scene in impartial silence: quadruple-checked, the craft sat ready to set out onto one of the grandest adventures in all the world and the only witnesses were my parents and I. I hugged them dearly. As much as I disagreed with them, I loved them. I love them still, as I write this. I placed the rosary-wrapped cross that my mother brought out into the hull and hung Saint Christopher's medallion around my neck. My mother wept. My father did not.

"I'll be back and all will be well," were the last words I spoke to them before I got into the craft.

"God bless," my mother said as I lifted off. My father stared silently. The sheep were out to pasture but, upon seeing the craft, they gathered by the nearest fence to watch. A pleasant audience. As I rose higher, the wind became mightier. Off in the distance, I saw Mr. Essayd of the *Gloucester Daily* arrive. He ran quickly and joined my parents below.

He was too late.

I rose skyward but kept glancing back at my parents. That was the last time I saw them.

Among the grass, I saw that white serpent from earlier. It slithered about before disappearing into one of the barns. My palm burned for a moment. I ignored it.

Everything below looked beautiful and small, it looked peaceful. Even though it wasn't.

II

THE WEATHER WAS fair. The clouds, like great white whales, moved leisurely across the azure sky. The aero-craft flew along smoothly. All its gages and measuring devices provided encouraging data. As an inventor, I was proud. As a scientist, doubtful. But as an artist, I felt that the Muses soared alongside me. The world below was beautiful. I know not how to describe Mother Earth's splendor, my friend, but it was as if I flew above heaven itself. Pythagoras wrote, "Leave the road, take the trails." I understand what he meant. I understand the beauty of the unkempt, the beauty of the struggle.

Nature's beauty is without equal: below me stretched endlessly the most beautiful woman in the world, her charms were that of a brilliant scholar and the most nurturing mother. This infinitely looping plane that we call home is the finest canvas of all. I would be a liar if I denied that I wept. Tears sat frozen on my cheeks as the cold wind whipped from the north. I apologize for the sentimentalities, but sometimes a man must make them know. Especially, when he stands on the edge of a void. We take this wonderful world for granted because we take ourselves for granted. We end, the world keeps on turning, but if we only cultivated our potential, our will to be more than just *the thinking animal*, then we too could keep turning with the world. A mortal's dream, of course, is to be immortal. The Eye has shown me the folly of such dreams.

After a few hours, I left the stretch of land we call the British Isles. Before me lay the chaos and churning bowels of the Ocean. It cared not for the dead Queen nor for the millions that starve on its edges. It fashioned and fed on itself endlessly. Those who have not seen this stirring mass, will not understand the terrifying beauty it incites. The Ocean is a sinking and rising graveyard. Its bowls hide more life and death than anything else on this planet. The ancient Greeks through Oceanus, the river, wrapped itself around all the world. I understand why they thought so. If from atop their masts all they saw was sapphire surfs, they'd think it boundless. I, too, from atop the sky saw no end to this mighty blue plane. An ungovernable vagueness stretched into eternity.

When the winds grew frenzied, I descended fifty meters, steadied the heat flow into the balloon, and set the rotor northwards. At this altitude, the wind was gentler. The sea salt scent rose from the churning whitecaps and cleared my sinuses. Ebony phlegm drained from my nostrils. London's coal smog, hidden away in my lungs, accompanied me even into the open ocean.

After course correcting the craft, I double checked my calculations. Night approached in mere hours, and with everything ensured, I decide to relax and do some reading. I brought Freud's *Die Traumdeutung*[10] in its native German and read it with great interest. It's a work of scientific imagination. Dreams are sustenance to the soul. They are the metaphysical nutrients we absorb as we slumber. Dreams are to us what the dark earth is to an acorn or a sequoia seed. They cultivate strength, determination, and a potential of infinite growth, but they also express that primordial malevolence within each one of us. They provide symbols for the unspoken, for the subconscious, for the true.

Unfortunately for me, I never finished reading the Austrian's thoughts. A squall shook the hull and the book slipped from my

10 *The Interpretation of Dreams,* 1900.

grasp. It struck the polished wooden banister that ran around the length of the cockpit, and fell into the waves below. Now the fish can read of their dreams.

I set all my meteorological instruments to their proper settings before dusk.

[Backwards and reverse starts.]

Night came quickly. It was a remarkable sight: the sky filled with swirling starlight and the glow of distant wreckages of doomed suns. There I was, a lone slab of flesh, floating through the domain of existence, looking up at the infinity above that reflected itself in the infinity below. A mirror staring at itself.

Reminiscing on that moment, on the calm before the storm, I cannot emphasize enough, my friend, how naïve I was to think I was looking into infinity. The dreadful Eye showed me what subsists out there in the eternal abyss. Infinity is an illusion. There is only an endless void and some dust on its way to becoming nothingness. All that exists does so to become something negligible. There is only one path for all living things, and it leads through the White Door from which the darkest light emanates.

[Backwards and reverse ends.]

[Drawn in charcoal, spirals of black doors populate the next two pages. In tiny print, the words 'Cin'Céline,' 'Cin'Adin' and 'Cin'Vooz' are written hundreds of times around the edges of the doors.]

Know this, my friend, when gazing into the night Ocean you hear churning and crashing and swirling but see nothing of what the Ocean wishes you to see. The Eye saw me then as I saw the Ocean. Insignificance drifts through it as much as it does through me. As much as it does through the end of all things. *Carpe noctem*![11]

Through that White Door, you can meet yourself and the

11 Latin for 'seize the night.'

remnants of who you once were. Madness plays there. And Malice. And Rage. A rabbit. A serpent. A wolf. All of them allegories for who we are and what we wish to escape from. All of them one, like mold: one root with a thousand crowns, a thousand selves.

The night grew cold. The gentle breeze did not help. It made the dampness of the open sea bite at every part of me. I lit the oil lamp, cooked some beans over a small stove top, and ate. The meal was delicious. It warmed my soul. I heated up some earlier-made tea. It warmed my body.

I gazed into the darkness for a long while. It reassured me.

After dimming the oil lamp, I unrolled the leather and wool tarp, which sat fastened to the railing, and extended it across two-thirds of the craft's cockpit. In case of rain or frost, the tarp kept the craft's innards dry and preserved heat. I took out two sheep skins from storage and covered myself with them. Within a few minutes of turning off the oil lamp, I fell asleep.

Up above the world, I had a very vivid dream of a deer that had gotten ill with wasting disease. The creature nibbled on some shrubs when out from the depths of the earth another bush appeared before it. As the animal sauntered toward its next meal, it grew emaciated. Its body withered away and that wonderful dynamic plumpness it had gained during the summer months vanished. Its coat grew mangy and lusterless. While this once magnificent creature listlessly walked on, its head lowered and lowered still until it simply hung there swinging back and forth like a sack of stones. Its eyes became bleached and blank. Showering the forest floor, drool and slime trickled from its mouth and nostrils. With each step the deer become less coordinated, stumbling increasingly, before falling sideways mere centimeters from the bush to which it had headed. From there the creature wasted away further: its breathing slowed and urine ran down its leg. The greenery around it faded, leaving behind a desolate plane of shadows. The deer took in its final breath and sunk into the black earth.

I lingered on the vision, the small dirt mound where the deer once lay. Around me, echoes of wheezing became ominous childlike screams. The deer begged for help from deep within its entombment.

When I awoke, a gentle drizzle came down from the overcast sky. Droplets rolled off the leather tarp and into a series of special water-collecting containers that lined the hull. I quickly got up, checked all my meteorological devices, and ate. The sun rose just after seven and, for a moment, transformed the rain into falling stars that plummeted from somewhere beyond the heavens. The universe's beauty reflected in my eyes. Slivers of radiance skimmed at a diagonal to diffuse into the vast sapphire plane below. The clouds parted slightly to reveal a valley of luminescence between two grim crags.

God himself guided me then. Moments later, I'd see to what end: ship wreckage dispersed upon the waves. Splintered wood and the remnants of a shattered mast lay battered by the surf. Clinging to a large piece of wood, a lone man floated among the horror. He saw me and, in English, screamed, "Help!" The wind carried his immediate bliss and fear. I descended, turned down the turbine, and steered the craft toward him. As I turned the wheel, which I reused from an old Åbo Skeppswarf steamship, I pulled a thick rope from a side compartment.

Upon seeing the aero-craft up-close, the man's face became bathed in pure awe. I hovered no more than five meters above him and flung the rope down. He caught it and, like a man possessed, climbed up. Upon setting foot on board, he collapsed and began shivering uncontrollably. I threw a sheep skin over him and, immediately, lit the stove.

"Warm yourself," I told him and he obediently relocated next to the flame.

I pulled up the rope, stowed it away, and concentrated on my guest. "What happened?" I asked. He looked at me blankly. His eyes were swollen and red. He looked like a fellow in his forties.

"Help," he whispered.

"You're safe. All is well now," I told him, and inquired once more about what happened. He remained silent, staring intently at the stove flame. After several minutes of trying to communicate with him—asking his name, his origin, if he's hungry, and the like—I gave up and turned towards my maps to calculate where I was. Having pin pointed my general location, about 450 kilometers north-east of Iceland, I was at a crossroads.

I knew that I was about to lose a day, but, at the very least, I'd get this man to headland and off my craft. I wasn't going to have anyone derail my expedition, especially not some shipwrecked mute. I ascended, adjusting several directional regulators, and piloted the craft Iceland-ward. Thankfully, accommodating winds carried us along. I hoped that in several hours, we'd reach land and, once this misstep concluded, I'd be headed north again. With the course set, I turned to the man.

"You must be hungry," I said.

"You and I are memories," he said with a Yankee dialect. "It's already gone. All is absent and adrift. All is a memory within a dream."

I assumed he was in shock.

"How long have you been in the water?" I asked.

Silent, he stared at the stove.

"I'll warm up some food and tea for you," I said, but as I reached for the pantry compartment, he grabbed my forearm and, terror-stricken, he said, "The Eye of Eyes. The Eye of Eyes." He repeated this without end.

[What follows is a single page of 'The Eeyeyeyeyeyeye […] of Eyes.']

I assumed he'd gone mad, his mind succumbing to isolation insanity. Perhaps all that he'd seen—all that I was destined to see—broke him. I knew none of this, of course. I was ignorant still. Instead, I thought myself burdened with a madman until I'd reach Iceland. Then I'd hand this wretched soul off to someone else to deal with. The goal was circumnavigation not madman relief. Reflecting on it now, I should have been a bit gentler, a bit more understanding, less ambitious and more sympathetic, but at that moment, the prospect of losing a day irritated me. A day, my friend. We rush into tomorrow without contemplating today, without enjoying its intricate simplicity. But a day squandered on aiding others is a lifetime of sustaining one's soul.

Ambition is a drug, an addiction of human nature: a man works on something he's passionate about, and others, seeing this passion and envious of it, for they have none of their own, act like logs in a clockwork, they try to halt the gears, try to make them crack, they make the mechanism toil harder until it shatters the logs into splinters. I didn't blame this man for being an obstacle. He is but driftwood in a mighty current, but how often does that happen? How often does driftwood become a dam that blocks the rapids? You're focused on a goal, whatever it may be, and along comes some human vermin intent on interrupting you, sidetracking you, distracting and dragging you into a maelstrom of what they need doing. It happens all the time. It is a pathology: some people exist as hurdles for others. Some people are literal gnats to genius: biting and annoying the gift, sucking dry the imagination and strength of those more ambitious than they.

"You're going the wrong way," the man said. "The things in the water do not approve."

He gazed at me as one does at a soiled vagrant then suddenly began wiping his hands, as if they were filthy, on the sheep skin. While doing so, he spoke, "We've ventured too deep into the unknown yet rarely tread the shallows of our own conscious, of our own being."

I watched him and grew nervous. Will this man murder me? What if I'm a day in this voyage and everything had already been compromised? A cold chill ran down my spine. I contemplated murdering this man before he did so to me. My mind ventured into very dark places, those small primeval holes in the back of the mind where the ape meets the serpent. If I'd just bash him over the head with a push pole and dump him overboard, all would revert to normalcy. One swing, one strike, right on the temple, or square atop the head. Some blood, a surprised moan, nervous shock, and a follow up strike, to make sure he's dead. Maybe one more after that.

"We're Iceland-bound," I said. "We'll find a coastal village. You can get help and I can be on my way."

"There is no helping me," he said, and for the first time he seemed sane. Sane, yet terrified. "It showed me too much, there is no going back to how things were. You just don't forget it. Not that…not seeing…and feeling…time itself gnash children into paste."

I remained silent. How do you respond to such words?

"It happened several years ago," he began. "My Helen and I, we were out on a walk across the Brooklyn Bridge. This man walked ahead of us. He stopped for a moment to look at the skyline. I wonder now what he was thinking. I wonder if he thought of all the man-hours it took to build New York. I imagine, because I don't know for sure, that he pondered every nameless man who gave his sweat and blood to make New York what it is.

"He went up to the railing and took in a deep breath. He turned toward Helen and I, gave us a smile and a nod, and just walked right off the bridge. It happened quickly. I made it to the railing just in time to see him smash against the water like an egg against a brick wall. And that was that. Here he was, this man, surrounded by the world and," he snapped his fingers. "Gone. How long did it took to shape this man? To make him *him*? The time, the endurance that his parents had to have to raise him. He must have gone to school where teachers taught him. He must have had a job. He must have had friends and relatives and lovers. He lived a life, struggled through it like all of us do, but he must have had something to show for it. Thirty, maybe thirty-five. He wasn't old. It took him that long to be, to exist, but it took a fraction of fraction of a second for him to end."

"Perhaps, it took him thirty, thirty-five years to end," I said.

The man nodded to himself. "The Eye replayed his fall in detail for me. Moment by moment, from different angels. From above and below. From within him and from a mile off the shore. It showed me the exact moment he connected with the water. The *exact* moment. Then it showed me all the men who fell before him and all the men who fell after him. They are still falling and they are still hitting the water, simultaneously. Always. Forever. It showed me the dream that is time. The infinite reflection that is becoming. This is wrong."

"Stranger," I began. "I think you are unwell. The shipwreck must have shaken your nerves—"

"We're heading south-west?" he asked.

"Yes."

"You need to be headed north," he said and in one swoop move, he tossed the sheep skin aside and jumped over the railing. He fell a hundred, a hundred and fifty, meter and made a whisper of a splash before the waves washed over him and he was gone.

"*They are still falling and they are still hitting the water, simultaneously. Always. Forever.*"

I tried to rationalize what had happened. First, I strained to come to grips with the fact that I just saw a man kill himself, even though, moments earlier, I contemplated killing him myself. Second, I recognized, that perhaps, this event is an omen of things to come. That thought made me feel rather uneasy. A spike in anxiety unbalanced me and I sat down out of a fear of falling overboard.

For the first time since leaving my parent's farm, I grasped that I was alone up here. A deep immobilizing melancholy overtook me. I spent the next hour or so watching the Ocean as it impartially moved to and from. The emotional maelstrom within me—the confusion, anger and dread—were completely irrelevant to the world. My head grew heavy and I became dizzy. I stared at my hands—the only tools that I had to get me through all that awaited. These soft hands of a man who's never faced true tribulation. I wanted my father to appear. I needed someone to help me. A dreadful screech of a misplaced albatross echoed from somewhere behind me.

After somewhat composing myself, I adjusted the craft's navigation mechanism to travel northwards again. Soon the melancholy returned. I fell into stupor and unintelligently, like a man in comatose, watched the horizon. I didn't want to be anywhere or feel anything. I focused on a blank sky, rather than scrutinize the tumultuous events that transpired. It was easier not to think. Deep down, I wanted to simply stop existing. I can't recall how much time had passed, but it seemed like too little and too much all at once. As the plume of shock began to fade, I reflected on the shipwreck's unflinching decision to, without as much as a second thought, fling himself overboard. There was no hesitation, only a mechanical resolution.

Often, I wondered if death extended only to our mechanical flesh and not beyond. If, in fact, like tools—be they a metaphorical shovel or rake or whatever—the muscles become weathered, strained or brittle; the network of blood vessels becomes corroded or overstuffed like sanitation pipes; the bones, like firewood left out in the sun, lose that sap of life, and harden into fossils. And with all this erosion comes madness. Sallust[12] wrote, "Harmony makes small things grow but a lack of it makes big things decay." Perhaps death is a result of a buildup of uncleanliness. Perhaps it's not an expiration of the body but entropy crystalizing over time on a plethora of functions. Perhaps, this present trend of melancholia

12 Roman historian.

among the bourgeois stems from too much leisure, from sitting hours at a time doing nothing, while the natural drive to move, to do, to create saturates their bodies with elements of entropy.

The cliché goes that a rock can withstand any storm but the constant dripping, drop by drop, will tear it asunder. The same goes for us. Time drips and we perish one drop at a time. The weather, the natural burdens we do and don't feel: gravity, pressure, moisture, heat, cold, etc. Add the plethora of rays and waves that the world and, in turn, we endure: radio, electromagnetic, ultra-violet, radiation, and the many thousands of strains we're not aware of, that we'll never know about. Perhaps aging doesn't kill us. Perhaps disease is a test upon the durability of flesh; an ever-evolving experiment to determine the optimal process by which nature can produce the perfect, the most durable flesh, so that the universe can continue being aware of itself.

Death, it seems to me my friend, is simply a reutilizing process. A way of nature admitting that its 'machines' are not durable enough. Its energy sources not practical, not efficient enough. From my engineering perspective, this seems right. This seems obvious. Every death is a recognition of a flawed blueprint and every birth an attempt at correcting the defects of the previous model. Any designer or mechanic can affirm: the process of improvement never changes, never stops. Death, too, will not change, it will only become more efficient.

To eradicate death is to say, "This right here, this form, this model, this version of mankind is good enough," and all improvements that nature is unable to grant us, we will grant ourselves. Yet a question remains: are we part of nature, and if so, is our meddling the meddling of nature upon itself through us? It is a difficult question, a nuanced question, yet the answer to it is simpler than you'd think. The Eye showed me. The solution begins at that White Door. It begins with a simple acknowledgement: all is decay.

[The following page is mostly blank. Written backwards, the words 'Soiled souls see no sunlight' sit centered on the page. A doodle of a spiral marks every corner.]

It must have been midday, maybe early afternoon, I can't recall now, when suddenly a black wasp landed on the piloting wheel. It surprised me to see an insect out midwinter, especially in the vastness of the sea. At first, I assumed it was a stowaway beast, until I realized that there were thousands of black wasps surrounding the craft. A swarm of ebony churned about like a whirlwind.

The creatures gave off a collective wail that moved through their ranks in a whisper. A sinister aura hung over the swarm. One of their number landed on my sleeve. Its body was without a doubt that of a wasp, but its face was human: gnarled and twisted like a prune. I swatted it away, and followed its flightpath into the distance, where an incredible occurrence unfolded: a great counter-clockwise-swirling puddle of color sat on the ocean. Along its edge, thousands, maybe even millions, of wasps circled about. The color gave off a horrifying growl. The puddle sank into an infinite darkness and became a swirling hole from which rainbow radiances extended like lightning. The whirlpool's corona became colorless and without form, there was simply nothing between the whirlpool and the ocean water that surrounded it. Waves did not venture near the maelstrom, instead they unnaturally bent away from it.

I realized that the position of the aero-craft shifted. I no longer flew north, but east, toward the swirling multitude. It was beyond my understanding. Perhaps, like a great interstellar mass, the hole had some form of gravity pulling everything in. Abruptly, the ocean became still. No waves crested for miles. Then I saw a small fishing vessel below. It, too, was drawn towards the hole. A great roar boomed from within the darkness. I composed myself and attempted to pilot the craft away from the pit. I put the engine on full blast, adjusted the directional turbine, and flooded the balloon with heat. A pathetic attempt at best. The engine itself acted as an operating aid; it wasn't a powerful enough prelusion system to counteract the influence from below. I watched the inevitable outcome.

Even though I did not expel any heat from the balloon, the craft descended at a steady pace. The pit exerted a strong pull on the hull, which creaked and bent from the stress. Afraid that the balloon and attached ropes, which held the hull aloft, would burst and snap, I reduced the flame and, to ease the severe pull on the aero-craft, released the pressure.

Being no less than a hundred meters away from the churning mass, a great lament burst forth from the cavity: screams of women and children assorted with visceral beast wails and cries of labored men. A booming otherworldly voice sounded all around, "*Et venit*!" and what resembled a gargantuan bird emerged from the depths. The thing flew near the craft. Its shape may have been avian but, in fact, it was a mass of naked human bodies gripping to one another. The thing must have been curious of the craft, as it circled around several times. The blank eyes and expressionless faces of the men, women, and children who composed its form gaped at me disinterestedly. Rot peppered their bodies. I crossed myself and, as if the creature itself gave off the horrid cry, the masses shrieked in unison. Before flying northwards, the bird swooped down to observe the boat below.

The core of my being shook with terror. I questioned reality itself: was this thing part of a nightmare or some hallucination of a distraught mind. I've read tales of lone sailors, of men lost in the wood depths, and of the macabre and indescribable sights that they had witnessed. In one such case, a lost logger[13] had come upon a grisly sight of his dead wife—miraculously young and alive—being gang raped by numerous insectile creatures while a gangly emaciated man giggled and quenched her thirst by

13 A tale reported in Alberta's Lake Louis newspaper, *The Daily* (1872-1907), dated May 19, 1889.

urinating in her mouth. Crusted with fallen tears, her eyes begged for death. Now the man spends his days near comatose, staring at door frames in Calgary's insane asylum. Such events have always had explanations: dehydration, exhaustion, or poisoning. But here I was, two days into my journey, and already I've encountered a madman, unexplainable gravitational phenomenon, and what, I could only deduce, was a hell-born bird.

The craft jerked downwards and the buzzing of the insect swarm grew near. The hull was almost atop the water. Its stillness unnatural to look at. The trawler was no further than twenty-five meters to my right. Panicked, its occupants ran around the deck trying to stop the boat's advancement toward the wasps. Waving, one man screamed something, but his words never reached me.

With the wasp's buzzing just behind me, I turned to witness the aero-craft's hull breaking through the churning mass of ebony wisps. Within moments, the swarm obscured my view. They were everywhere. Human-faced wasps crawled all over my body. Their thin insectile legs prodding my flesh. Instinctively, these predators hunted and searched for any orifice, and upon finding it, they forced their way inside. These tiny terrors overwhelmed my mouth, ears, and eyes. A symphony of screams echoed around me but soon it became muffled by the toll of creeping insects and buzzing wings. While I choked on their hard shells and willowy legs, the skittering sound of wasp crawling over wasp reverberated throughout my head. My tongue fled deeper into my throat. I gasped for air.

Suddenly, I felt a pleasant warmth. The last thing I remember seeing was a massive eye with a thousand flagella fanning out of its back, orbiting around it like a boundless halo. Beyond that there were only wasps in my eyes. As they desperately crawled into my skull, their exoskeletons pressed against my eyeballs. I fainted from the pain, from the panic.

I awoke face down on a wet black dune. After coughing up

a great deal of sand and phlegm, I sat up and, instantaneously, became dizzy. The world was a blur: black sandbanks became ebony waves, the sky a massive pulsating drone of violets and scarlets. My hands resembled talons. I closed my eyes. It helped. The vertigo faded. I wiped the sand off my face, and cleared out of my nostrils. I stood up. Black sand covered every part of my body. I felt movement in my stomach. Something slithered throughout my guts. The buzzing of wasps filled my ears, then I felt something creeping up my throat. I vomited sand and wasp wings.

A black plane stretched into the horizon. There were gentle hills here and there. A few bizarre shrubs populated the sparse landscape. Strange gelatinous clouds drifted in the east. What looked like flagella or tentacles or serpents—I do not know for sure, because they were all three of those things at once without being any of them—slithered throughout the clouds.

My aero-craft lay nearby. The collapsed balloon sat undamaged. The hull was fine, but black silt covered every inch of it. Someone moaned beyond the deflated balloon. I circled around to see the trawler from before turned onto its side. It, too, was sand-garbed. Like a killing blow upon a wounded beast, a large gash ran across its stern; torn beams and loose boards littered the ground before it. Facing the boat, an impaled man dangled limply from one of those shattered beams. Some thirty meters away, facing up, another figure lay next to a bizarre shrub.

[Backwards and reverse starts.]

I ran towards to body, but upon noticing the bearded man's cracked skull and the accompanying halo of blood that encircled it, I stopped. With a sigh, I walked over to him and checked his pulse. He was dead. I momentarily observed the corpse's strange beauty. If not for the circumstance, the blood halo seemed angelic. Its circumference almost a perfect circle. Through the film of silt, his face appeared tranquil, a true blessing for all his disquiet and toil faded with the passing of his soul. Slicked back, his hair lay half-hidden in the sand and gave off the illusion that he was one with the terrain, a sort of fading blemish upon the Earth's face.

A loud *thud* sounded behind me: the door of the ship's small superstructure swung open and a man emerged. Limping, he slid his way down to the gangway on the port side and disappeared from view. Thinking to aid him, I made my way toward the boat but the angler emerged from beyond the bend as I reached the hull. His tibia protruded from his scarlet-soaked trouser.

He spoke something in Norwegian or Swedish, I'm not sure which. "We need to get you to a doctor," I said. As I made my way toward him, he leaned back against the boat and slid sideways onto the ground. A strange sound, like something moving through thick slime, resonated behind me. I turned to see that those gelatinous clouds had moved much closer to us. Their flagella moved about the sky like eels on a hunt. The horizon vanished behind a curtain of strange rain, which was gray, yet glimmered like a puddle of petrol that one sometimes sees at the train yard.

[Backwards and reverse ends.]

The Scandinavian began to weep in agony. I rushed toward him but as I was about to reach him, he looked past me and began to scream in terror. The rain did something horrifying: it discombobulated the dead man and the nearby shrub. I don't know how else to describe it, my friend, but with each rain drop, the flesh and the plant matter spiraled upward in a double-helix then became a luminescent crimson mist that looked like suspended paint flakes. The organic matter simply decoupled from the whole. The man and the plant became one with the rain, and before the crimson mist disappeared into the downpour, it formed a perverted blueprint of the human nervous system mingled with that of a plant.

A strong odor of sweetness blended with rancid meat washed over me. While my reason tried to comprehend this horror, my instinct to survive took hold. I'm ashamed to admit, but I ran past the screaming Scandinavian and up a short dune. Halfway up the incline, I glanced back at the man. He tried to stand on his broken leg but fell. The discombobulating rains washed over him. As he became organic double-helix vapor, his screams changed into ominous musical chimes.

III

AS I REACHED the top of the dune, a small town of about a dozen black-bricked buildings came into view. The rain was at my heels, I could hear it strike the sand behind me. Yelling for help, I ran toward the nearest structure. The door to a small house opened and a middle-aged woman waved me on. I ran as fast as humanly possible. She must have recognized the force of my stride, as she moved aside, disappearing beyond the doorframe. As soon as I stepped onto the open-air porch, my strength failed me and I tumbled onto the hardwood floor inside the house. The woman quickly closed and bolted the door behind me.

The rain washed over the house. I could hear it pelt the roof.

The woman knelt beside me, and although she spoke an altogether strange half-Romance, half-Asiatic language, consisting of an overabundance of vowels and nasal intonations, I could understand her. "Are you all right?" she asked.

"Yes, thank you," I answered and she gave me an odd look, as if aware that I too spoke a peculiar and different sort of language from hers, and yet here we were, able to communicate with one another.

She helped me up. Having steadied myself, I realized that beside a table and four chairs, the room in which I stood was completely bare. A sole black candle sitting on the table illuminated the gloomy sight: black walls, a lone door to the north, another one to the west. Two windows to the east and between them the door though which I fell through. It struck me as strange that there were thick iron bars on the windows, while above one of them, attached to pair of rollers, which could be lowered and raised by a chain, set within adjacent industrial tracks, sat a thick metal sheet with a horizontal slit to look out through. The other window's metal sheet was down and over the frame.

"Where you from stranger?" the woman asked and without pausing to hear the answer, she produced a wooden bucket from under the table and began wiping the black door on the western wall with a damp rag. In fact, the doors were so pitch black and alike to the walls that one had to strain his focus to really distinguish them from one another.

"I'm from Snowshill, England, but originally from occupied Poland," I told her.

"That sounds like a far-off place," she said. "I'm sorry for not offering you anything to eat or drink, but I have to clean the doors before they disappear. You know how it is."

Perplexed, I stood silently.

"Don't be a stranger, stranger. Please, make yourself something to eat. There is bread and water on the table." I looked back and where once there stood nothing, sat a bread basket with a jug of water, and a plain glass, beside it.

"Thank you," I said and introduced myself.

"That's a fine name," she replied. I waited for her to introduce herself, but no such introduction came. I sat down, poured myself a glass of water, and ate the stale bread.

"Where am I exactly?" I asked after a long and awkward silence.

"This here is Orphora, at the edge of Abyssum," she said.

"What country?"

"Oh, a normal one," she said then continued to ignore me. Her focus lay on the precise cleaning of that door. After wiping the door's frame, she wrung the rag and wiped the door, after which she wrung the rag again, and wiped the frame. She did this repeatedly. Her dedication to this mundane task was unlike anything I've ever seen. She didn't just clean it as one does a piece of dusty furniture on a Saturday morning. No, no. She delicately went over every part, every indent, every ridge of that door from the very top to the very bottom. The washing of this entry and exit point seemed like a very carnal task to her.

When she reached the round handle, she'd wring the rag per usual, then gently, almost erotically, caress every inch of the knob, move her face real close to it, as to watch her handy work, and give off low groans that bordered on whispers. What delight she took in her work, what satisfaction. While her fingers glided and tightened over the door knob, her breathing hastened, and her lips cured up into a suggestive smile. She indulged the four screws that held the handle in place in the same fashion. First, she moistened her fingers in the bucket, then gently polished each screw, rubbing the suds into the crosshairs. As the froth ran down the door, she gave off a naïve giggle and bit her lower lip. Then she tenderly wiped everything off. With a satisfied pant, she returned to wiping the door and its frame.

Having eaten several slices of bread in, I don't know how long, while this woman nonchalantly—or to be blunt, erotically—cleaned the door, seemed an odd sort of happening, especially when an unattended stranger sat in her home.

"That rain and those clouds," I began, hoping to start a conversation. "They had—"

"Rain like rain," she said, giving me one of those looks that one gives when caught or interrupted in performing some sort of carnal task. "Clouds like clouds," she added, blushed, and, after a long pause, added, "You're just lucky you weren't caught in it, otherwise you'd be the rain."

She stepped back from the door and admired her handy work.

"This one won't vanish anytime soon," she said then knocked on the door. Out from beyond it, emerged a middle-aged man dressed, much like her, in all black. His face was weatherworn. He was bolding.

"We have a guest, Wife," he proclaimed.

"We do indeed, Husband," she said, and, as if doing it for the first time, gracelessly kissed him on the cheek.

"Hello, sir," I said, shook the man's hand, and introduced myself. "I crash-landed outside of town in my aero-craft and I'd hope that perhaps you'd—"

"Dear Wife, can you please bring some food for our guest," the man chimed in and awkwardly placed both of his arms on the table.

"Of course, dear Husband," she said and walked through the western door into pitch blackness, but as soon as the door closed, she returned carrying a plate of roast chicken, potatoes, and sliced pickles. The aromas of paprika, garlic powder, thyme, rosemary, and sage spread like summer warmth throughout the room. As she placed the dish before me, my mouth watered at the prospect of delighting on something warm. "Thank you," I said. She stepped back, and, smiling, the two of them gawked at me like jesters. I looked at the plate then back at my hosts. Their grins seemed to elongate yet quiver, giving me the impression that the very act of smiling tortured them. They gave off an aura of uncanny disquiet. The man's pinky trembled. I was about to ask if everything was fine, when the man urged for me to eat.

"It's impolite for me to eat when the two of you aren't," I said.

"We ate before you arrived," the wife said.

"Big meal," the man patted his belly. "A lot of food."

"Utensils?" I said.

They exchanged concerned looks, before the wife said, "There they are," and there they were, next to the plate. I felt a fool, but

I swear to you, my friend, she never brought them with the food, they just appeared.

"Yes, of course," I said and ate in silence. They continued watching me as if I were some distinct museum exhibit or a rare beast at a zoo. "It's very good," I said to dispel the silence. They nodded synchronistically. The man's gaze focused on my mouth. He seemed to take immense pleasure in my chewing. His eyes swelled with satisfaction at each bite. The woman, on the other hand, absorbed my tearing of the meat off the bone. With each jab of the fork into the chicken, she clenched the rag, which she never relinquished, and give off slight yelps of excitement, very much like a little girl does when she sees an endearing pony or puppy. Feeling rather uneasy with the situation at hand, I began, "I assume you're wondering who I am and what I'm doing here, especially at such a late hour? Well, a short time—"

"Time?" the husband inquired. They both frowned.

"Well, I flew—"

"Time," the wife repeated as if it were the very first time speaking the word. A faint smile spread across her lips. The man's hand began to tremble.

"Yes, well…"

"Yes, well time," the man said.

"Time is a well," she said to no one in particular.

"Wells are deep," he began. "The deeper the well, the longer the time that we fall. To fall into a well takes a long time. All wells fall in time."

I said nothing. The three of us looked at each other like cretins at a carnival fire. I wasn't sure if I should speak or wait for them to engage first. Of course, if I knew that they were both dead, I wouldn't have said anything at all, but the Eye hadn't showed me that yet—I haven't been *blessed* by it—so, instead I did the only polite thing I could and, like an adolescent with a windmill tongue, told them of all the strange episodes of the past couple of days. They stared silently, barely blinking, continually grinning. I concluded my little yarn with, "I hope you'd be so kind as to help me recover the craft in the morning?"

"Yes, we'll do that when the rains pass," the man said.

"Thank you," I replied and ate my meal to the accompaniment of rain gently tapping against the roof. Upon finishing the final morsel of food, the wife, like a hunting praying mantis, snatched the plate and bread basket off the table, and, leaving behind the water jug and glass, swiftly, went through the western door to just as quickly came out and, without another word, begin cleaning the northern door with just as much passion as she exhibited toward the western one.

"Ha!" the man laughed unprompted. "You remind me of a fella I once knew. He spoke of flight, time, and strange places."

"Is that so?"

"Everything always returned to the idea of the soul with that fella," he said then paused and looked at his hands. "In time, I used to be a historian," he said in monotone. "I..."

The wife reached the northern door's knob. She began panting.

"The soul is a sliver of the universe," he began, "that constantly wishes to be reborn. It thirsts for otherness. That is where envy stems from. Envy is the soul wanting to undergo a transformation. That's why it's often said that when we die, we feel a sort of euphoria that is beyond anything that we have felt in life. It's the soul finally getting what it wanted: something else, a sort of apartness from what it once knew. But upon rebirth, it yearns again for transformation, and, concurrently, subconsciously, faintly remembers its past existence, which materializes as that strange sensation that we sometimes feel: an anxious melancholy, which pulsates from the back of the head throughout the whole of one's flesh."

"I know the feeling," I said. "It's a strange sort of self-doubt. It makes you question everything, *especially*, when things are going well."

"Especially then," the husband said. "This fella, he thought that there comes a time when the worth of one's soul is exhausted by the universe. He referred to that exhaustion as *languor,* an integral aspect of one's final life in the cycle of death and rebirth. In languor, the soul is drawn toward suicide. Having experienced the universe through eight higher lives, in the ninth, and final one, (this fella believed that that each soul had nine *higher* lives—meaning lives as a human being—and thousands of lower, in-between ones, such as being a blade of grass, an insect, an animal, and the like), the soul becomes bored with life, but knows that it hasn't yet experienced the greatest and most dangerous of acts: suicide.

"Thus, it kills itself, and destroys all the wisdom and knowledge that it had acquired over the thousands of lives that it had lived. This is *the* rule of all cosmos. The universe had learned all it could through *that* soul, and now that that soul is oversaturated with data, it needs emancipation. It needs an end. It needs release. This always happens during this ninth higher life. Do you feel that you're living your ninth life?"

I sat silently pondering what he had said. As the wife's cleaning of the north door reached its crescendo, I began, "I'm not sure what languor, as he defined it, feels like. Perhaps it's a lengthy lassitude of being. Perhaps, it's a perpetual resentment that leads to sadness. Perhaps, it's madness masking as misery. I don't know, but I do know that this is not my final existence. I'm not even sure if this is my first life." Later, the Eye would show me that, in fact, this was the last of them, the ninth, and that, for me, there came nothing after. No heaven, no hell, no afterlife. I'd return to what I was before my birth and remain as such till the White Door opened.

Do not worry, my friend. The path ahead leads me not toward suicide. However, I've done things that suggest that I'm finally at an end, at some sort of conclusion to this life of mundane triviality. The truth is that, since puberty, my soul had eroded. Like every blooming adolescent, my will toward rebellion and introspection multiplied during that time, it made me angry, downhearted, and longing for something that I couldn't put my finger on. It made me aware of the brittleness ahead. And when it passed, when I reached my twenties, I did not adhere, as most of my friends had, to the demands of civilization—a wife, children, career, engagements with polite society. Instead, the black fires of Thanatos awoke in me. "Create and die," they whispered. "Create and die."

[The following page is colored crimson. No words appear on its surface. In the middle, draw in black ink, sits the Eye of Horus.][14]

My friend, I feel as if my past and present dwell in a realm of nonexistence. There lingers on my mind this feeling of floating without movement, of falling without wind on my face, and that when the fall ends, when the innards of my soul end their floatyness, I will realize that, like seaweed battered by the waves, I have existed in an illusion of weightlessness. I fear the feeling is a lie. I believe we feel fabrications. That, like that seaweed that floated before, I'm not floating now, I'm not falling now. Instead, I've washed up on some massive seaside stone and have, for these many years, been drying up. Dying. That the feeling of rebellion, of angst, of melancholy, of adventure are the symptoms of my rotting soul, clues to the putrefaction of this final life. I feel life had been a haphazard lie.

"There have always been nine families in this town," the husband began, "and there will never be a tenth. Nine is as many as this land will support. No more."

"If you're concerned that I plan on staying here to start a family, trust me, I won't. I want to fetch my craft, fix what needs fixing, and leave."

A great blare, as if made by an organic horn immersed in

---

14 Ancient Egyptian symbol which represents well-being, healing, and protection. It is believed to have protective magical powers.

slime and spittle, bellowed outside. I saw movement of a contorted silhouette beyond the barred window. My hosts acted as if nothing was the matter: she continued washing the door, while he gazed at me with those intense brown eyes.

I heard a serpentine voice in my ear and felt someone standing behind me. Startled, I stood up and turned around to find no one there. "*Aestimatus sum cum descendentibus in lacum*," the voice whispered again.[15] Spreading down from my ear throughout the whole of me, a bizarre emotion ensnared me. An awareness of being a fraud, of someone or something looking right through me and seeing all my flaws, all my shortcomings, all my sins. That no matter what I did, no matter my successes and wins, no matter the outcome of my life, the echo of the judgment of my peers and the ceaseless torrent of condemnations from people I have never met remained. Imagine your whole *being* judged as you stand naked before an endless tribunal, not of Men, but of disembodied eyes. Never blinking, always adjudicating, always heaving upon you their way of seeing the world. This damn feeling of impostorism remains even now as I write to you, my friend.

I felt movement beyond the eastern door, an emotion pulsated from it. I felt something looking at me through the entrance, through the walls, from above and below. That over-the-shoulder feeling of being prey to something's unwanted gaze proliferated throughout me. I needed to know what it was that was gazing into me, what it was that judged and neglected me simultaneously. Was this paranoia? Was this an unconsciousness knowledge of my own failings? Was this unexpressed rage hammering at the gates of my subconscious wanting to flee the confines of stoic reason? Was the thing beyond that door a suzerain of my thoughts, actions, desires? What becomes of the judgment of a judge when no one hears his

---

15 Latin: "I have been counted among those, who climb down into the grave."

ruling? Why do we fail to be happy with who we are, but are quick to take the opinion of others about our account as truth? Why the questions? Why the doubt? Why the hell were these contemplations consuming my mind?

The house shook but my hosts didn't notice—maybe they didn't care—because they went on pretending that all was well. There was another great blare of the horn. A female scream rang out from beyond the northern door.

"She arrived yesterday," the husband began, "around the same time you arrived today. She was lost. Spoke of very strange things, of undead wyverns and spheres of floating corpses. She's resting now. Gaining her strength back."

Children's laughter hid in the rain, followed by a greater laugh of some*thing* from the darkest of fairy tales. The house shook again. The open window shutter slid down with a crash. A murmur of voices seeped into the room from the outside, followed by demonic merriment that played without end.

Just as the wife finished washing the northern door and returned to scrubbing the western one, a young woman rushed out from beyond the northern one. She hissed like an adder and ran toward the entrance, unbolted it, and swung it wide open. The rain fell hard, yet, I saw it with my own eyes: the trajectory of the raindrops bent and spiraled around one central, invisible point. Something unseen unnaturally pulled the rain toward it. The senseless laugher originated from that unseen thing. For the first time, fear flashed on the couple's faces. Their expressions bent and twisted with horror. Almost instinctively, like primordial beasts, they rushed the woman. The husband's hands became shackles around her wrists. However, her madness was too resolute. She tossed him over her back and jumped onto him like a lion does onto a wounded gazelle. She hissed. Her porcelain teeth snapped at him. He slid sideways, kicking at her with his boots. The wife grabbed her by the head from behind and pulled. They fell back together.

"Close the door," the husband yelled at me. The wife wrapped her arms around the woman's neck and squeezed. The wild one gave off a peculiar noise like that of a rabid beast at death's door. I rushed to the door and just as I was about to slam it shut, I stopped. The rain seemed to be breathing. Something called for me from the downpour. First came a horse neigh, then the whisper of my name. Something sat at the threshold of the rain just beyond the porch roof—at the exact spot where the rain met the dryness. The spiraling drops gyrated faster and faster still until they burst into a blaze.

Friend, my description of this thing does no justice to its dreadfulness. There were eyes upon eyes and eyelids upon eyelids and eyes within eyes and they too held eyes inside them and amorphous irises emerged and formed strange porous humanoid flesh, but that too was devoured by ravenous eyes that like froth multiplied into different eyes. And while this infinite genesis occurred, a singular black pupil watched, judged, saw, ate of the image, ate of me.

This too I saw: humanoid things that stood no further than a meter away yet appeared blurred as if observed from behind a pane of steam-slicked glass. When reflecting on these entities, a Freud quote comes to mind, "They are not dead like persons who have died to our sense, but they resemble the shades in the *Odyssey* which awaken a certain kind of life as soon as they have drunk blood."[16] It was as if these things strode out of Claude Monet's *Impression Sunrise*: they were nothing but blurs of secretion, eye, dermis, and stain—corporeal, yet soulless.

[The middle of the next page holds a crudely drawn Eye of Providence,[17] with a quote from Voltaire[18] underneath, "The mirror is a worthless invention. The only way to truly see yourself

16 Freud, 216.

17 An eye, often encased in a triangle and surrounded by divine light, meant to symbolize God's watchful gaze over humanity.

18 Pen name of French philosopher, François-Marie Arouet.

is in the reflection of someone else's eyes." Below the quote, sits a column of nine eyes which shrink in descending order from topmost to lowest.]

[Backwards and reverse starts.]

We're all just stains on a burning canvas: fading splotches and twisted amalgamations of evolution and savagery held together by a bond of culture. For all the values and morals that we espouse behind pulpits, upon daises, and at breakfast tables, we are nothing but shades to the ideals that we so fervently encourage. Hypocrites and false men, scions to the obscurities in the woods rather than idyllic philosopher kings. How often have we ran, umbrellas in hand, through rainstorm-swept streets, passing silhouettes in the dampness? How often were we unsure of what we passed? Were they people? Are we?

Slavic folktales advise that when an intense storm comes through everyone should move indoors. No one should venture outside for *widma*[19] roam the rains in prospect of looting Men's souls. These silhouetted phantoms move about in the deluge like bloodhounds, pursing those stupid or unfortunate enough to ignore the forewarning. Those unlucky few who venture into the storm, never venture out of it. After the tempests pass, pierced upon the topmost branch of a dead tree, their bodies—now dry, soulless husks—swing at the edges of ancient forests or field-fenced copses. What I saw outside that door were *widma* and things beyond even the scope of folklore and the supernatural.

Upon feeling my gaze, the apparitions withdrew into the breathing rain. The eye mitosis decelerated then burst into a grand luminosity that became a great eye so massive that it was impossible for me to behold all of it at once. However, seeing but a sliver of it obliged madness to wash over me. The Eye of Eyes' omniscience perforated every cell of my being and an ocean

19 A spectral creature from Slavic mythology.

of all the world's injustices past, present, and future washed over me. Wrongs of every sorts deluged my corporeal mind. My legs quivered from the inconceivable weight. It was torture to see the voluminous deceits, wounds, and vices of the world. To see rich men steal from the poor and receive no punishment for their thievery from unjust and corrupt judges, made me see red. There were oriental children sowing shoes under sheet-metal roofs while affluent sportsmen stood on podia spewing duplicities pietism about equality and freedom. I saw the pittance that plumbers and coal miners and workers of every profession collect from their toil sitting beside mountains of currency that financiers *created with their pens,* by assurances of prosperity to hopeful, naïve souls.

[Backwards and reverse ends.]

What justice is there when millions starve and perish of the elements while devilish criminals—murderers, pedophiles, rapist, and the like—sit in warm jail cells fed daily with medical aid available at a cough's notice? What justice is there for a raped child when the villain's dubbed an invalid who needs treatment for his molestation disease? What of the working man who toils for twelve hours a day to have all that he owns be taken away by a government repossessor, a bureaucratic boor, because the system is mammon and theft? Where is justice when two brutes kill a bloke but they hang the pauper and fine the usurer? Where is justice when the piranhas in Parliament raise taxes on the citizens then increase their own rewards on the following session? Where is justice when a villain is lionized, while a hero is christened nefarious? Where is justice when arbitrarily a fraud takes you to court but it is *you* who pays for the trial?

Quick are men to blame others, but quicker still do they deny blame when it is set before them. There is no justice, only fables of it and false tongues who express them. But the Eye, this authoritative soul beholder, showed me the truth of Justice. It displayed her bare, with no scale, no sword, no blindfold. She held in one hand a satchel full of gold, in the other a whip. Her eyes were churning vortexes of night that drank in all light, all goodness, all truth, while out of her mouth spewed out the black bile of falsehood.

A jolt of power ran through my eyes and down into my timorous legs. I heard my brother's voice, "No sparks, no fire." I shut and bolted the door then collapsed onto the floor. I hyperventilated while trembling from head to toe. Children's laughter and the screaming of the wild woman waned until it became nothing but a whisper. My trembling faded with the laughter and the screams. As the wife helped the woman through the northern door, the husband grabbed me by the shoulders and, in one swoop movement, lifted me up to my feet and led me to a chair.

"She had told me that she came from Sazanthia,"[20] he began. "She spoke of a civil war being fought there. Along with her child, she escaped the carnage, but just when they thought they were in the clear, walking along some path in the woods, rogues struck and they fled into the forest depths. She ran till her feet were bloody and bruised. 'I held my daughter's hand so tight, it turned blue,' she told me.

"After serval hours of running and hiding, exhausted, she collapsed onto the forest floor. Unfortunately, she fell where the ground was loose and undone. A sinkhole opened and, as the ground gave way to nothingness, they plunged into an abyss. She woke up in the Black Plane: dunes and wasteland around her. She was lucky to arrive just before the rains did. Delirious and dehydrated, with her daughter gone, most likely dead or rearranged by the rain, she fell into a psychosis-induced slumber. She had an outbreak of lunacy earlier in the day. The voices in the rain must have exasperated her further."

As I was about to question what it was that I saw out there

---

20 A mythological land—often referred to as a Dream—found in numerous esoteric texts from the Middle Ages.

in the storm, the wife emerged from the solid darkness of the northern door, and coldly spoke, “You must sleep, stranger. We have an extra cot.” She leered at her husband who, like a shamed schoolboy, blushed and quickly looked down at the floor. Without another word, he went through the western door, but before it could close behind him, he emerged holding a cot and a dull yellow blanket. He placed the plain, narrow mattress in the corner between the western and southern walls. Then without as much as a ‘bye,’ he disappeared into the darkness beyond the western exit.

The wife began cleaning the entrance door into the house. “Why do you continuously wash the doors?” I asked out of curiosity, but she ignored me and went on wiping away. I set my shoes beside the wall and laid down on the cot. “What we did in life, we continue doing in death,” she said to no one in particular. Feeing frail yet heavy, I turned away from the candle light toward the wall, and drifted off into slumber. “The doors mustn’t vanish,” I heard just before falling asleep.

I dreamt vivid dreams. I was a young boy in Poland. It was late summer and, along with my parents, we were picking orange potato beetles off the leaves and stems of the potato plants we sowed earlier in the season. We did this every year; the beetles arrived to eat the plants and ruin the crops. Some years there were a few hundred beetles, others a few thousand. Some years there came a single wave, in other, two or three, but there was never a time when no beetles appeared.

We’d tie these small sacks to our belts then we’d pick the beetles off and throw them into the sacks. We’d squish them as we tossed them inside. By the end of the day, smelling of bitterness and digestive acids, our hands glistened bright yellow, stained by beetle guts. All these years later, that acrid smell clings to the inside of my nostrils and the memory of beetles crawling over my fingers remains.

I remember arriving at the fields in the morning to beetle

pick: the lively green potato plants lay hidden under a scuttling mass of orange. After hours of picking, I'd glance back at the rows of cleared stems and felt satisfied by the simple fact that life blazed through the green leaves, that they continued to flourish. Rarely, but it did happen, I missed a beetle or two on a plant that I thought I'd cleared completely. Thankfully, my parents were quick to catch the runaways. The beetles concealed veiny wings under their armor. Often, they'd know—at least that's the way I justified it to myself as a child—that we were coming for them, so they'd fly off and land on a plant that I'd already picked clean. I'd act a bounty hunter: track the fugitive beetles and squash them between my thumb and pointer finger.

The picking of potato beetles was a Sisyphean task. Our field was one of a thousand, and what beetles perished on our field were quickly replaced by beetles from another. They'd arrive in smaller numbers, of course, because everyone around us—farmers and their families—beetle picked, but always these orange thieves make their way over to us. Always there were plants we'd reach too late. Leafless stalks crawling with orange were a reminder of our failure. Sometimes we'd get help from our neighbors and, in turn, we'd help them the day after. Such was farm life: anyways helping and being helped.

It was still nighttime when I awoke. The rains had passed. While the wife wiped the northern door, the wild woman, with her back to me, sat at the table watching the candle's dancing flame and storytelling. I pretended to sleep and eavesdropped on the woman's tale.

"…the roots of the tree are its most important part," she said. "All of their time is spent in the darkness of the earth, and, like tentacles, they spread forth throughout it to absorb and pilfer what nutrients they can to relay it back to the seed. The earthbound roots make the beauty and greenery above possible. No tree springs from the light. In fact, the light kills the seed that sits within its grasp for too long. The light dries the seed, it saps away its will to grow and become a tree. Light is a thief of potential.

"A child, too, is like a seed: living in the darkness of its mother. It, too, appropriates and absorbs only to become—like a seed on its way to full bloom—a person. A child that blooms is a wonder to behold, it is life giving itself prospect. Yet, we never give credit to the roots in the darkness, instead we praise the canopy above, the canopy of lies. We never praise the unseen. This is the problem with mankind: it sings hymns to things it's seen, never to things *a priori*, never of the unchangeable, untestable, unseen and unsound. Man fears those things. As the old saying goes, 'We fear the unknown,' the hidden. But it is what we fear most that feeds us the best, that nourishes us in abundance, that makes blossom the human tree."

The wife gave off a shrill, insectoid noise full of buzzing and clicking, a sort of blend between a cicada and a cricket.

"Yes," the wild woman said. "Before I found this town, I wandered the Black Plane and upon its ebony sands came across a very old man. He was completely naked. Skin hung off his bones like it does on an overripe peach. He was a living example of the cruelty of aging.

"When he saw me, he turned and began begging for help. Thinking him in dire need, I walked toward him, but he sprang forth like a predator and grabbed me by the arm. There was something visibly wrong with him. His skin was raw, but in moments become like a dry hide. Terror-filled eyes begged for death. Suddenly, his grip loosened and he grew older and older still. After giving off a feeble shriek, his bones tore through his skin and he fell apart like a fort of twigs in a gale.

"A pile of bones and rot lay before me. The bones became dust and that, in turn, became a gelatinous grime. The grime became a tiny mass and soon that became a fetus and this fetus quickly changed into a babe. The babe became a toddler. The toddler became a child and so on until a middle-aged man stood where once there was nothing. In a terrified voice he spoke, 'Aid me, please. I know not what happened. Years ago, I hiked through the Appalachians when a great storm came around, and, within this tempest, I saw a great flagella-haloed Eye. Simultaneously, I felt a terrible insignificance and a massive weight of judgment upon my shoulders. I ran deep into a cave until the darkness solidified and it swallowed me whole. Thereafter, I materialized here in this plane. And then came this rain and…'

"By the time he'd articulated this point, he was back to being the old man from before. He felt his body wither. Weeping madly, he gave off a horrid shriek and fell upon the ground on all fours. It did not take long for him to became rot again. The decay moved and again it became an embryo, a fetus and so forth, until I saw a babe. I saw it and I ran away."

Making insectile noises, the wife continued cleaning the door.

IV

WHAT MAKES HUMAN beings special when compared to other animate beings? Everything lust: man for woman, stallion for mare, reptilian bull for reptilian cow, tierce for hen, drone for queen, stamen for pistil, yet, human lust is sin. Or is sin human lust? Do we have ideas or are we conduits through which ideas become tangible? Take revenge as example. Retribution wasn't born of us, rather murder as a potential act invaded us in the form of the idea of vengeance that then led us to tangible murder. The idea needed feeding. By killing we fed it. Same goes for lust. Lust needed nourishment, and we gave it what it wanted. That is the difference between man, and, say an echidna, one is a tool of ideas, the other an experiment in-progress to becoming a tool. Something is thinking, but it doesn't mean it is us.

Immortality is thinking.

[Covered with infinity symbols bursting from a single black eye in its middle, the following page's corners have been singed. On the left-hand side edge, going from bottom to top and written in pen, sits a William Blake[21] quote, "If the doors of perception were cleansed, everything would appear to man as it is, infinite."]

Having finished her tale, the bizarre woman departed through

21 An English romanticist poet, artist, and printmaker.

the northern door. Going from one end of the room to the other, the wife continued washing the doors until sunrise. Plotting out what I must do to flee whatever hell this was, I lay awake most of the night. Intuition recognized that departing this place was vital to the stability of my sanity. My friend, the longer I lay there, the more corrupted I felt. Some invisible parasite, some force, gnawed at my soul, at my conviction. The danger of losing my faith, my courage, grew with every passing moment and I feared that once sapped, I'd not only believe in the strangeness around me, but that I'd believe in anything. To believe in anything is interchangeable with believing in nothing. Only the dead believe in everything and nothing at all. I clasped my hand around the Saint Christopher medallion my mother gave me and, for the first time in years, recited the Lord's Prayer.[22]

It wasn't long until the husband entered via the western door to shake me. "Wake," he said.

"Yes, yes," I replied.

"Good," he said. "Let's get your boat."

I nodded in agreement, stood up, and, without a breakfast, went outside. The wife glared at me as we departed. Something in her posture and movement changed since last night. She seemed more hunched, more feral. With the rains gone, the area became bleaker, lonelier. What the downpour hid, the overcast sky exposed: a derelict village where homes resembled blocks of coal. Beside their rectangular form and small windows, nothing suggested that they were manmade. Peppered about, strange curved spires, resembling black whale ribs, stretched toward the sky. There were no trees, no shrubs, no plants of any kind within the town's border.

To reach a large stone arch in the center of town, I followed

22 A central Christian prayer from the New Testament through which Jesus taught his followers how to pray.

my host down a narrow path hidden between two houses. I saw men and women—one per window—stare at me through the metal bars. Their eyes were sunken, the faces emaciated. An atmosphere of uneasiness hung about the whole of the village. Nowhere did I see a child.

We walked past the arch and stopped at the nearest house. My host put his hand on the door and it seemed to vibrate a little. A peculiar ringing in my ears accompanied the arrival of the home's owner who opened the door and greeted us with silence. He was a short man with grey eyes and a long nose. He wore all black. A woman, presumably his wife, wiped down a vague door on the opposite end of the entrance. The man must have noticed my gaze, as he quickly shut the door behind him and stepped outside. My host explained that I came from a distant place and needed help retrieving my boat from beyond the dunes.

"Wisps and ghosts are memories of broken minds," the man said while looking me over.

"Hello, neighbors," a voice sounded behind us. A heavyset man with a missing eye and warped hand appeared from beyond a corner of the house. The two of them said nothing. I replied, "Hello."

The husband introduced me. "Jan, this is Tailor, and, my neighbor here, is Teacher."

"How do you do?" I asked out of politeness.

They stared, not so much at me, but at the space that I was occupying. Tailor turned to Teacher then spoke, "I have made plans. One day, when we return, I will make the most beautiful dress in all the Dreams. And everyone will look upon it with awe. They will feel the soft fabric under their fingers and speak praise of the fine stitching, the wonderful and detailed ornamentation, and it will be the finest dress they have ever seen. I have made plans."

"Plans you have made," Teacher said and the two of them stared at one another for a few awkward moments. Without another word, Tailor walked away and disappeared beyond the corner of the house.

"How big is this boat?" Teacher asked.

"It's not a boat," I said. "It's a balloon with a fuselage—"

"How big is it?"

"About five meters long. It's not large."

Teacher walked off. Both the husband and I followed. We passed a large farmhouse, a well, and several smaller abandoned buildings on the far side of town, beyond which stood a long, black stone building that pulsated with a malicious aura.

"See if that works?" they both said in unison.

"Yes, that works," I said.

"Yes, but go and see," they said. We stared at one another for a moment before I reluctantly walked off toward the building. The entrance and front façade sat crusted with parched barnacle remains. What looked like sunbaked arthropod exoskeletons and appendages littered the ground. They crunched loudly when I walked atop of them. I peeked inside. It had once been a beautiful stable. Along a broad central aisle, spacious gated stalls ran down the length of the whole structure. Once decorated with detailed horse carvings, the gates became weathered and moldy. There was more than enough room inside to house the aero-craft. As I turned to return to my host and his neighbor, neighing and the sound of horse hooves in charge echoed through the stalls. Startled, I looked back. The length of the building was empty. No horses. No danger. Unhinged at the top, the back door swung sluggishly in the draft.

I looked back at the two men. With their backs to me, they stared at something in the village. Then came the neighing again. I felt a need to go inside; it became essential for me to make sure that there were no horses hiding in the stalls. Why? I don't know. I just needed to see, much like a curious cat does before it's torn by an enemy. I stepped into the shadow. As my eyes adjusted to the gloom, I noticed a riding saddle sticking out of the dirt. I knelt and pulled it out of the arid earth. Carved into it with something sharp, a crude symbol of three halos surrounding an eye sat prominently at its center.

A bray sounded right beside my left ear. It gave me such a fright that I spun around and sprang backwards deeper into the stable. To my surprise, there was nothing there. Again, no horse. With a sigh of relief, I looked around. The stables themselves were decrepit, rotting, and falling apart. The roof was dotted with holes. Rays of light shot down like spotlights in the gloom. I spotted a dilapidated carriage in one of the stalls. Only one of its wheels was still functional, the others rotted away years ago.

I walked on but saw nothing of interest until I reached the other side of the structure where, hidden in the corner, sat a battered wooden horse,[23] not the carousel variant seen at carnivals and fairs, but the torture device. Without a doubt, the *chevalet* was a Spanish donkey variant: a large triangular 'body' with attached shackles and a small wooden splint on the side to ensure that the tortured didn't fall off the whole, and four sturdy legs, from which hung frayed rope. I slid my hand along the 'body' and noticed a black stain in the middle of the triangle where, like iguana spines, five smaller triangles lay: this is where the victim sat and the weight of their own body cut into the angled wood. What pain hid in this simple wedge-shaped cut of wood? What screams it heard? And why was it here? A shiver of scrutiny ran down my spine.

Something moved in the peripheries. I turned to see a silhouette of a famished horse at the other end of the stable where I had come in. It brayed and entered one of the stalls. The gate shrilled from corrosion. I walked over to where the horse had gone but stopped right before opening the gate. My gut churned with dread while my limbs disobeyed me. Suddenly, I felt inescapable fear.

23 A triangular torture device designed to use the subject's weight to inflict pain upon them by lowering them onto it.

Every part of my body told me to leave: my breathing quickened, a cold sweat dampened my brow, and my hands quivered. Nonetheless, I reached for the gate as a wasp flew past me. The memory of the swarm crawling into my insides diminished my fear, and the disgust I felt waned my curiosity. The wasp buzzed about before flying throughout the stable. I followed it, crossing the structure, again, and passing the wooden horse. The insect flew outside and off beyond a large dune at whose base sat the stable.

I walked back toward the village. With their backs to me, Teacher and my host awaited silently. "The stable will do," I said as I walked up to them. They stood as still as statues. Their eyes were closed, but under their lids, they were gyrating. I cleared my throat. Their eyes shot open. The husband asked, "Should we collect your boat?" I nodded.

We walked back across town and up the dune behind my host's home to reach the aero-craft. The fishing boat and my craft sat as I left them the night before. Where the three Scandinavians once lay grew bizarre plant-flesh hybrids: pulsating shrubs with crinkled flesh for bark and what looked like fingernails for buds. Like moss, patches of hair grew out from the bark. A slanted nose here, a twisted ear there. I crossed myself and felt Saint Christopher's medallion under my shirt. Once the known is consumed by the unknown it becomes the uncanny, which leads to an existential panic: to the known dying. Seeing what had become of these fishermen altered the way I thought about being. It made me fear what I will become. Buried in the dirt or burned to ash, seas of grass and oceans of trees were going to feed on my essence.

[Backwards and reverse starts.]

"Does the rain do this?" I asked my companions.

They stared at me blankly.

"Does it reconfigure living things? Reorganizes carbon based life?"

They ignored me completely and began rummaging through

the fishing boat. Not knowing what to do myself, I climbed into the boat's entrails through the hole in its hull. When my eyes adjusted to the darkness, I saw numerus nets flung along the floor, the walls and ceiling were overgrown with a scaly moss that glistened whenever any sunlight peeked in through the cavity. I realized that this was the Scandinavian's catch. The moss grew as a mass of fish fins, tails, and eyes. The piscine conglomeration was breathing. Covered in a thin film of slime, the mass moved like a sentient lung, gently inflating and deflating at regular intervals. The rain did this. It must have. The terror I felt in my stomach was nauseating. From the corner of my eye, I noticed movement. A silhouetted figure stood in the doorway.

"*Farlate*," it said in a winded gasp then, like a pile of sand, fell apart into a heap. As I moved toward it, the sand disappeared in-between the cracks in the floor until nothing remained. I felt dizzy and couldn't catch my breath. I fled the boat. When outside, I put my hands on my knees and, with the heaviness in my chest gone, took in deep breaths. I had to leave this purgatory.

My companions stood over by aero-craft waiting for me. I joined them.

I checked for any damage that I might have missed last night. Everything seemed fine. After placing the deflated balloon into the fuselage, we pushed the craft up the dune. I took one more look back at the boat. It sat there like a long-abandoned house, begging for a prayer, begging for absolution, begging to be forgotten. The buds on the flesh shrubs opened to reveal flowers that resembled veiny hand palms. I felt as if they were reaching out toward me, asking for help, begging for memory, for an escape.

[Backwards and reverse ends.]

We pushed the craft through town. Tailor emerged from beyond the same house corner as before and, without saying anything, helped us push. The town's residents watched impartially from beyond their windows. We pushed the craft up to the stables but just as we approached its entrance, the three of them stopped almost as if by instinct. I sensed a deep sense of hesitation on their part.

"Come on," I said. "Just a few more meters." But they remained still and silent. Fine, I thought and pushed the fuselage inside by myself. Deciding to fly off as soon as possible, I began supply and instrument checks right away. All my supplies were still there. I wiped off as much of the black sand off the hull as I could, and swept the inside, including the thin film that obscured the gages, valves, and measuring devices. The thermometer was cracked. The mercury had drained from it. This was a rather big setback when it comes to data collection. I quickly found the hand thermometer I had in the supply compartment. It wasn't the industrial sort of device that sat cracked among the dashboard, but I had to make do. Remember my friend, at that point, I still thought my circumnavigation was only halted temporarily. If I only knew. I triple checked the gages and recognized that the meteorological instruments needed recalibration. They showed impossible numbers and measurements, for example, the barometer read, 19.3 Hg, while the compass kept on spinning counterclockwise.

With everything calibrated, the only thing that remained for me to do was to fill the balloon, but, with the corrections and maintenance checks taking so long, I had to do so the following morning. I felt good after everything had been accomplished. For the first time since I've seen the sunrise the day before, I felt content and, even, happy.

Those emotions faded almost instantly when I recognized that I had to spend another night in this dreary town. I could have left there and then, flew off with the sunset, yet something had a chokehold on my decision. It's difficult to describe, but I felt as if I couldn't leave until the following day, that it wasn't *right* to leave now, that I wasn't allowed to do so by a kismet of some sort. As if the thing in the rain implanted within me a destined procrastination. And yet I knew that wherever I was and whoever these people were, they were not personages with whom I should remain for long. Their presence—my presence in this place!—acted like a lamprey upon the soul: weakening my resolve, digesting my faith, nourishing itself on my inaction.

I heard another horse neigh. Everything around me seemed still. What dust floated through the air appeared to be suspended in a solidity that disapproved of motion, of choice. Another neigh and the world's motion returned. I decided to check the stall into which I saw the horse go into earlier. I pushed the gate open and stepped inside. Something cracked under my foot. It was a dry and brittle horse skull. It looked as if it had been there for a great long time. Two horse skeletons lay in the corner, one of which, I assumed, was a mare, the other, smaller one, her foal. Their flesh had rotted away long ago. What remained was bleached memory veiled within their bones.

A shiver ran down my spine. What optimism and courage I had had vaporized. I felt trivial standing at the maw of ever-devouring time. With equine corpses at my feet, my mind spontaneously went to a scene in Cervantes' *Don Quixote*[24] when the titular character looked upon his horse, Rocinante: "Having completed his work, next he proceeded to inspect his old steed, which was bony and blemished as a trollop, *qui tantum ossa et pellis fuit*,[25] yet the mount surpassed Alexander's Bucephalus or the Cid's Babieca[26] in his eyes." Long ago, I read that horses symbolize courage and strength, and Cervantes decided to use Rocinante, this emaciated and malnourished mustang, as a symbol of a diseased courage, a courage that stems from madness, from a distracted dementia. A

24 A Spanish chivalric novel written by Miguel de Cervantes.

25 Referring to female prostitutes of the 14th century: 'nothing but skin and bones'.

26 Famous warhorses.

blemished courage leads to a sullied future. So, what did these dead horses before me mean?

The suggestions that of my mind put forth terrified me. I observed the detail of the foal's ribs—their worn strength and forgotten potential—and a severe melancholy overtook me. The suicide's words rang in my head: "How long did it took to shape this man? To make him *him*? The time, the endurance that his parents had to have to raise him." The whole scene made me ponder all these babes whom now lie in shallow graves, of children whom were innocent 'till death. Seas of potential lie buried under mounds of black earth. What happened to those souls? To what end were they reborn to die? For what purpose?

Somewhere in the distance echoed neighs assorted with the laughter of children. A memory of my brother and I as youngsters danced around in my skull. Summertime. A copse in rural Poland. Farmland all around. Drying under the high noon sun, mounds of hay lay spread about. "Jan, Jan!" my brother yelled as he ran toward me holding a freshly broken off silver birch twig. Upon its leaves sat a small emperor moth caterpillar. Its green greener than the leaves, while peppered along the length of its body, in rows of six, orchid-purple globules shined like amethysts on a tsarina's necklace. Long black hairs stuck out like lashes out of its body. We consumed its beauty and delicacy, the enchantment found within its tiny form. "It's ugly!" my brother said, squashed it in-between the leaves, and ran off laughing, eager to find some more bugs to kill. Only the cruelty of nature surpasses the cruelty of children. That moment bonded us in some vague way. As all shared moments do. True, we grew apart since then, but it doesn't mean that our roots are as untangled as out cranial canopies. There came another neigh, this one assorted with a concealed weeping of children.

The noise faded quickly, replaced with a buzzing from within the mare's skull. A wasp emerged from the eye cavity. It circled above my head, then, like some gothic specter, flew *through* the stable wall. I gave off an irritated sigh and went back to the craft. The irrationality of this place annoyed me. The urge to leave immediately intensified. As if this place felt my desire to take flight, the sky became dark and bleak, blocking what light shined through the holes in the roof. There was a low rumble outside. Another storm was incoming. I grabbed a pencil and notebook from the craft and hurried outside.

The three men were gone. Pulsating, veiny clouds slowly sailed across the sky. I heard ocean waves break against the shore and wind whirl just beyond the dune behind the stable. The sea is so near? I pondered this and quickly ascended the dune to see what lay beyond.

"Come!" the husband yelled from below. "A storm is approaching."

The sky grew darker. Its purple veins intensified in hue. The sound of the sea faded. A great bellow of fury rang from above. Something moved through the clouds. It was time to go. I walked down to my host. "Is there a sea beyond there?" I asked pointing at the dune with my thumb. He looked up at the ridge with utmost seriousness, and with distressing intensity spoke, "There are no seas here. There is only sand." He paused, his face overcome with intense anguish.

"Is everything alright?" I asked.

He gave off an insectile click followed by a stern, "Come."

As we entered my host's home, the rains came. In the dark, the wife washed the northern door with a maddening intensity. Her spouse lit the lone candle on the table, bolted the entrance and rolled down the metal sheets over the windows, then walked through the western door. That was the last time I saw him.

The downpour became more intense then the night prior. The rain fell sideways belting the windows. I could see movement between the slits in the metal plates. Otherworldly noises sounded at random. My stomach grumbled. It has been a whole day since I ate. I regretted not having eaten some of my provisions at the craft. I sat down at the table, setting my notebook across from the candle. I tried to start a conversation with the wife, but she either didn't hear me or didn't care to speak to me. Instead, I opened my notebook and wrote, reflecting on the events of the past couple of days.

Beside recording the unusual events thus far—the suicide, the ocean hole, the Black Plane, etc.—I contemplated on something that Saint Augustine[27] mentioned in one of his journals. He discussed, in Latin, that if one letter is changed in a word, for example, filth (*caenum*) into heaven (*caelum*), and vice versa, you have a completely altered perception of meaning. Depending on one's mental state, this slight alteration can skew or correct one's whole awareness of reality. A small difference to a word can become a vast difference of the whole.

Now if this small alteration is to be applied to actions, think, my friend, what little feats, such as giving alms to a beggar, reading a few pages every day, or, simply, smiling more, can do the soul. Men aren't willing to make little changes for they fear the greater outcome: the likely possibility of changing who they are now into the best self. The now-Man is comfortable, he's safe and at ease, but the Man-in-transformation is unknown and provoking, he's an unknown quotient. Men's actions can only be changed by their words, by their capability to wield those words as Augustine did: with purpose toward a fair end.

Words and action are the building block of the near perfect Man. Too many people use empty words. Too many say 'Umm,' 'Yes,' 'True,' 'I agree' or some variant on these terms. What a waste of breath. Men must learn not to interrupt each other with words that don't mean much. They must speak with intention. Their words must be actions in sound waves. Imagine speaking to a top engineer, the best industrialist, or a mighty philosopher king, do

27 Augustine of Hippo: 4th century philosopher, theologian, and bishop.

you think he'll say 'Uhum' in the middle of your statement? He will listen and respond cerebrally.

[The following three pages are mostly blank. Written in pen, a single word sits in the middle of each page. They go, in order: 'Be. The. Words.']

"It is clean," the woman proclaimed. Without as much as a glance my way, she opened the western door and entered the solid darkness beyond. That was the last time I saw her.

The next few hours were long. Time felt like a lighthouse flare seen from a vessel cutting through choppy waves upon a foggy sea. It sped up here, it slowed down there. It felt uneven and distant at one moment only to become clear and near in the next. The room's black walls and doors became a corporeal cell holding an incorporeal prisoner. Shadows danced in the darkness to the tune of the candle's unseen, unheard fiddle. The faint light from beyond the slit in the metal plates formed spiraling tunnels that led nowhere and everywhere at once.

I felt omniabsent.

From their individual solitude to their collective becoming as me, every atom I possessed presented me with their journey. They passed through distant stars that no longer glimmered, millions of organisms that no longer breathed, and unspeakable number of celestial spheres that no longer spun. We are each recycled death. Our atoms were once Buddha's, Shakespeare's, Christ's. Genghis Khan, Saint Francis, Beethoven, van Gogh live within us, speak through us, and when a particular event, sound or image stirs within us an appropriate emotion, it stirs within their remnants too, and awakens their bursting will, creativity, and passion. We are reincarnations of reincarnations going back as far as Nāḥāš (נחש)[28] and even long before him.

---

28 Hebrew for 'snake.' Also, a name appearing in the Torah that identifies the Serpent from the Garden of Eden.

Stuck with mutable time between these four black walls, I peeked at the rain and watched the candle's flame interchangeably. I expected to see my hosts back at any time, but they never returned. I grew hungry and thirsty, and decided to knock on the western door to ask for some water. I walked up to the access but paused before acting. Something suggested that knocking here would do me ill. I stared into the door's blackness and for a moment felt ethereal. My body became air. My mind became somatic. I felt the darkness, the flame, the sound of the rain. It all felt immaculate. I knocked, but you'd never know it by just listening, because my knocking was noiseless. It's as if I knocked on air.

I knocked again and silence echoed. The engineer inside me wondered if the door was made of some special sound-dispersing material? But the child in me knew…A shiver of uncanniness descend down my spine. This wasn't right. I reached for the knob when, suddenly, the northern door opened, and the bizarre woman walked out from beyond carrying a glass and a pitcher of water.

"Hello," she said and placed the glass and the pitcher on the table. "Thirsty?"

"Yes," I said and sat down.

She poured me a glassful. I thanked her.

"You're welcome," she said. I drank it all in a single gulp.

"One more?" she asked.

"Yes, please."

She filled the glass without taking her eyes off me. The candle light accentuated her beauty. She was a comely woman, no older than thirty with shoulder-length wavy brown hair. I drank of the second glassful then set it aside.

"Are you feeling better?" I asked.

"Yes, much better," she said. After a short locking of eyes, she stood up and peered outside into the rain. "Another dreadful night."

"Yes," I said. "All they have here is rainy nights and overcast days."

"I've always loved rainy days," she said looking back at me. "I used to sit beside the window at home: cup of hot tea in hand, a good book, my lap covered by a warm blanket. I'd get lost in the stories. Tales of romance and betrayal, loss and vengeance. Agony." She paused and looked back at the rain.

"Sounds like a fine way to pass a volley," I said.

"It was," she said, then glanced at the ground. She returned to the table, observed my face for a moment then sat down. "What have you been writing?" she motioned towards the notebook with her head.

"Not much," I began. "Just reflecting on the past few days."

She reached for the journal. I didn't pull back. She took it and flipped to a random page where a pencil-drawn landscapes of the British shore sat. She flipped to the next page: the Atlantic Ocean draped in sunlight, and the next.

"These are good," she said with a smile. "I especially like this one," she showed me my rendition of a sunrise in the fog.

"Thank you," I said. "I think of art as a child of mine. It developed from something crewed and unrefined into what you see there."

Her smile vanished and she became still. After closing the notebook, she slid it my way. We shared in the silence.

"Where are you from?" I asked, trying to dispel the unease. She glanced at me then at the candle flame.

"I'm from far away," she began. "I got here not long before you did." She considered my face then, without breaking eye contact, moved her chair beside mine. Our legs grazed against one another. The energy in her eyes had changed, she became predatory. "I went to the bogs with my child. We were going to gather peat—cut it, shape it into blocks, lay them into piles to dry in the sun. This way we'd have fuel to burn to keep us warm when winter came."

My passions flared when I realized that her blouse lay open. My eyes rushed to her bosom. She must have realized it. "Winter are frigid where I'm from. Warmth is hard to come by." She smiled encouragingly and pulled her chair up closer to me. Her legs slid in between mine so that her knee brushed against my groin. She parted her legs slightly so that her outer thigh slid against my inner one.

"I didn't have money to buy coal and it was something to keep the boy entertained," she said and quickly glanced down at out touching legs. "While I cut and formed the peat blocks, he carried and placed them in mounds under the sun."

She rubbed her leg against mine and kept on gazing into my eyes with a seductive predation.

"There was a great rumble from deep within the bog."

I became erect.

"We both turned to see, what I can only describe as, a great rift of light." Her eyes smiled with recollection. "It spread a great deal of pleasure throughout my flesh."

My erection pushed against my trousers.

"My toes curled, my nipples hardened, my intimates grew moist, and my skin became a hive of gooseflesh. An immense pleasure spread throughout every inch of me."

She noticed my erection. With a coy gleam, she gently caressed it through the trousers.

"Then *poof* I ended up here," she softly massaged my glans. "With my child gone, I wandered the Black Plane for a day? A week? A month? Who knows? Who cares?" She paused to intentionally nibble at her lower lip. "But the pleasure remains. It's here with me at all times." She rubbed her abdomen. "And it wants more. It needs more seed. It demands it."

She unbuttoned my trousers, took the tip and, kneeling, brought me plenty of pleasure with her mouth. The indulgence of the flesh is the most wonderful of hedonisms. Pleasure pulsated from the root into every extension of my being. It eased all pain and made me forget hunger and sorrow. She was exquisite. Her mouth radiated a warm delight up my abdomen and into the heart of my very soul. Her softness brought out my denseness. Every movement of her tongue led the stiffness of my soul closer to the ultimate release.

When it came, the delight of ecstasy coursed through my flesh like a mighty current. Upon climax, I opened my eyes to see a gigantic bloodshot eye peeping at us from beyond the window. A mighty blare shook the house and, quickly, my mind went from desire to terror. I attempted to stand up, but she pushed me down and continued to take my seed as it arrived. Greedily, she licked everything up. When she tried to force the fullness of her tongue into the tiny opening of my member, I kicked her aside.

She became feral and tried to tear me open. I sidestepped her lunge and shoved her back when she snapped at me with her teeth. My member burned with soreness. Swiftly, I made myself proper and buttoned my trousers. Standing on all fours like a wild beast, she smirked maliciously, leapt, and landed by the door. A chilling insectile drone whirred from her throat.

"Don't ever speak of this," she hissed. Her face became haggard and weatherworn. As she screamed of returning her children from the past to the present, her speech changed constantly between differing voices. "There will be many of them and they will inherit the lands far and near."

Her face decayed rapidly until it resembled a timeworn corpse. Like a spider, she scurried towards me, tackled me to the ground, and clenched my neck with one gaunt hand.

"Save me," she begged. "Save me from the Gray Windcaller's plan!"

She brought her lips near my ear and, in a soft whisper, spoke, "Hollow eyes within the empty wolf skull watch life seep away, drank in by a shoal of lampreys that are the memories of who we once were. Blessed are the dead, for their flesh will never taste the star fire from above—from the tendrils of Cyn."[29]

She licked my face then threw me against the wall. Like an earwig, she scurried to the door, tore it open—hinges and all—and, screaming in agony, stood up. A great hollow blare echoed all around the house. The foundation shook. She took a step toward the threshold. A great lamentation—moans, weeping and the like—commenced and grew in intensity to such a degree that I, too, became tearful.

Suddenly, her belly swelled as if a hundred hands were pushing out from within her. She tore off her blouse, turned toward me, and began laughing manically. She looked as if nine months pregnant. Hand prints appeared all over her abdomen. Children's laughter echoed from within her insides.

"No!" she screamed then hysterically began punching her belly. The lamentation outside grew louder. "God save me!" she cried while thrusting her fingers into her bulging abdomen, tearing asunder her own flesh. On a psychological level, Freud's words best describe what I saw, "Like so many other young women, she was by no means happy when she became pregnant, and admitted to me more than once the wish that her child might die before its birth; in a fit of anger following a violent scene with her husband, she had even struck her abdomen with her fists in order to hit the child within. The dead child was, therefore, really the fulfilment of a wish, but a wish which had been put aside for fifteen years, and it is not surprising that the fulfilment of the wish was no longer

29 The line originates from Nostradamus' manuscript discovered March, 2020 in Salon, France. The manuscript (untranslated at the time of the publication of this book), titled *Of the Sky-Torn Masses*, holds several prophecies about the shattering of the sky, the splintering of time and space, and the rising of the dead to tear down all of civilization. The manuscript is estimated to have been written between 1563-65. How a line from a lost manuscript found its way into Jan Cichy's writing, remains a mystery.

recognized after so long an interval."[30] Pregnancy: the horror of life-giving.

A great sound of the sea crashing against the crags of some nearby shore rumbled outside. It shook the earth and the sky with how loud it boomed. Abruptly, as if a vacuum swallowed all sound, all became quiet. And then, from within this chilling void emerged a noise of dreadful lamentation and the coming of a great tide from afar. The danger felt real. The coming tsunami resonated in the rain. Whatever was coming came with a torrent of terror and tears.

"There are no seas here. There is only sand," the husband's words echoed in my head.

30 Freud, 139.

V

IT HAPPENS AT least once in a person's life: a great sadness merges with an immense fear, sorrow meets dread, tears meet screams. Fear becomes a virtue. Be it a parent's death—the child grief-stricken and contemplating how to exist in a world void of their father or mother—or an incurable disease—facing the end of one's own life in a world blooming with it—the sadness of fear[31] permeates our being and clings to us like a tick. We become weary of others, of new situations. Depending on the impact of the sad fear, we become slightly or greatly more resentful of the joys of others; for how can they understand, how can they not feel the sadness of fear as I do? And it burrows into us like a woodworm into a mighty oak. It saps our will, it decimates our hope with holes, holes that it fills with more fear, more sadness, more regret. Sadness of fear becomes fear as virtue. Those who are afraid believe they are better people than those who are not, and will subconsciously look to proliferate fear to seem more virtues. Cowardice becomes widespread because it's seen as a righteous asset.

The human soul is so expansive, so infinite, that it is unable to correlate all its content. Within us live thousands of islands ignorant of one another, unaware of the endless blackness that

31 Jan uses the Polish term *smutek strachu* implying that fear itself is saddened by said melancholic events.

separates them. Paradoxically, the soul is an unending tunnel, its walls our bodies, and the sadness of fear is what tests the tunnel, the walls. It pushes out from within and in from without. However, it's also the endless blackness that existed before we were born and was passed down to us from our ancestors. Sadness of fear is the proxy of suicide. It is the emotional fountainhead of the act of self-termination. Since its genesis, the human race has battled against it, and must continue to do so until the White Door is open.

Sadness of fear is a rotting stork carcass sprouting daffodils.

There was this flash of dark light. Sad fear poured into the room. Everything blazed yet, simultaneously, it was shadow-shrouded. The woman struggled all the way until the end. She continued to beat her belly until the veiled light enveloped her and, like a splintering tree during a lightning strike, she shattered into a thousand fragments.

The building shook and something tore the whole east wall from the rest of the house. The rain became like a sea turned on its side. Waves came to and from. From the rain's depths, radiant tendrils emerged followed by a great Eye within, what resembled, a flower of labia minor petals—fleshy and skin sheathed. One petal overlay another forming multiple layers of petals that expanded beyond my perception. The Eye sat within three golden halos. An eye within an eye.

I peered into me. It did, too.

[Backwards and reverse starts.]

I stood beside myself yet gazed into all of me: my flesh, my mind, my soul. The Eye touched everything that my gaze did. Every part of me, corporeal and metaphysical, felt its scrutiny. I heard it in my head as a distant wind. I felt it on my flesh as a numb crawling sensation not much different than when one's limbs 'falls asleep.' I tasted wine mixed with ash. I smelled fresh resin becoming amber. The two I's—the me beside and the me nearby—merged. Flesh became spirit, spirit became flesh and together they became Jan Cichy. A beautiful woman and handsome man appeared beside me and placed their hands on my shoulders.

I saw night, light, and grayness play within an unfathomable orb of striking light. It hummed like celestial luminescence through a bottomless gorge. I felt the light contemplating my thoughts as they flowed from my mind in the form of notes and images to form a halo, which encircled my head. All sorrow, all fear, all worry left me. Only contentment remained. The pulsing light made me feel sufficient in ways I cannot explain. It made sure that I knew that, at the end of all things, everything will be fine. All will be well. The end is inevitable.

An unpleasant looking skeletal man in a four-eared rabbit costume, a beautiful woman with long, flowing auburn hair and evergreen eyes, a man dressed in black with white porcelain skin, and a woman garbed in what looked like suspended embers stepped out of the light. Beside the ember garbed woman, they all observed me for a moment then faded away leaving her behind. Since the foursome appeared, she had stood askew and away from me. I never saw her complete face, only the left-hand side.

[Backwards and reverse ends.]

She smiled a melancholy smile and put out her left hand toward me. She held a music box in her palm. The other three figures appeared and reached for the music box. Before they could touch it, comets and suns and stars and galaxies burst forth from their chests and combined with the music box to form a star-churning being. The being and the music box separated. Above the music box stood a featureless creature no larger than a child. It was humanoid and all white. On the left-hand side of its head sat a vast swirling black void. The four figures stood inside it.

The music box cracked. The ember garbed woman gave off a dying gasp and faded from the humanoid's eye. Instantaneously, all sorts of white animals with pied feet fled from within the music box's fissure. The white figure faded. Along with an endless lament of Men, stems and branches and roots emerged from the break.

Where once sat the music box now stood a titanic tree of rippling light and darkness. Fruits of every sort of plant burgeoned from its branches. Then they transformed and became heart-shaped: slimy, fleshy, beating. They dropped from the branches. In the time it took for them to fall and hit the ground, they metamorphosed into a variety of beings. From tiny winged Men to gigantic wyrms, all of them grew as trivial as grains of sand when a black fruit fell, landed as a man but quickly became an enormous wolf. Strong and powerful he grew, with curved fangs as sharp as an angel's arrowhead set within a ravenous maw capable of consuming the stars.

An immense winter storm encircled the wolf and it howled so loud that all existence heard it and shook. Out of nothingness, thick chains emerged and wrapped themselves around its body. They pulled the creature down from the storm. The brute struck the ground with such a force that heaven-high waves of earth rippled out from where it fell. The beast howled and became emaciated and bony. While its physical form appeared frail, its eyes blazed with raw determination: full of hate, radiating terror, plotting its revenge. The wolf sank into the soil and a vast city of towers and strongholds grew out over where it sank.

The city burst like a bubble.

A violent war between land and sea, between dry and wet, unfolded before me. These primordial forces smashed upon one another to create a plain of mud, which bubbled and simmered and cooked until all sorts of creatures crawled out of the mire: men, beasts, and fantastical creatures I've no words to describe. One of these beings was a tiny golden salamander. Like a blacksmith's hammer to a sword, the might of fire and rain and wind and earth honed it until it became a dragon so immense that it stood before me like a mountain stands before a grain of sand.

The dragon roared and out of its jaws flew out thousands of dragons of all shapes and sizes. They all flew past me like a wave. The might of their wings created such a gust that I had to shield my eyes. The two figures beside me stood tall against the wind, their hands firm on my shoulders. When the dragons passed, a little moth and an earwig fought on the floor before me. Their battle was brutal: they bit and tore at one another with hateful intensity. *Smash!* A great metal boot squashed them. The boot belonged to a dead man garbed in an astounding armor of feathers and lights. Every emotion known to man entered my being. I felt heavy. The beauty and ugliness of who this stranger was and what he wore overwhelmed me and I fell to my knees.

The dead man smiled. Fingers peeked out from beyond his lips then two hands forced his mouth open from within. The porcelain-skinned man in all black emerged from his mouth and, like a slug, slid down onto the floor. As he stood up, both men were stabbed from behind by a handsome man with kind eyes. They turned to ash which clung to the handsome man's hands and stained them black. The man materialized a needle and thread from thin air then sowed his lips shut. As he did so, the Golden Dragon attempted to smite him, but the man was nimble and steadfast. He slew the dragon and from its massive corpse burst a small village that grew into a city, a nation, and finally, an Empire with towers and walls and great pyramids and heaven-bound spires. A million men slew a million more men and the Empire became war and blood until nothing remained but a field of corpses.

The stench of death hung heavy over this endless cemetery. Its silence broken intermediately by the buzzing of flies, the cries of vultures, and the howling of wolves. As vermin consumed the carcasses, they burst into fiery columns that stretched and disappeared into the sky. The flames burned bright, charring the earth and the sky to such a degree that only the man with the sown lips remained.

He noticed me and frowned. Becoming barbed wire, the thread keeping his mouth shut hardened. The barbs pierced through his flesh. He squirmed from the pain. Tears ran down his cheeks becoming a group of faceless men who stood around a tenement-sized black cauldron. Bubbling and screams reverberated throughout the cauldron. The rising steam resembled wisps of anguished spirit. The liquid within the cauldron boiled uncontrollably and a young girl emerged from it. A plethora of tattoos moved about on her flesh. They depicted horrible things: monsters, acts of murder and rape, hell spawn and the like. After a moment, the ink on her body became a singular splotch that burst into a hundred butterflies that soared upon her flesh. A lean ashen specter in a torn white cloak grabbed her by the neck and pulled her back into the swill. I heard her lamentation from within the simmering brew.

A deep chill came and frost crept up my body. The two figures beside me stood tall through the blizzard. Their hands on my shoulders. Warmth descended from their palms and throughout my flesh. I felt immense warmth though surrounded by the worst winter imaginable. One by one, the figures surrounding the cauldron fell dead until only four remained. The four watched the cauldron grow silent and cold until it became as still and reflective as a mirror. A dim light shined from the tranquil liquid. It illuminated the four's faces. They were all identical: young green-eyed men. They noticed me—much like Sown Lips did—and after kindly nodding at me, they stabbed their sides with glimmering blades, and plunged into the draught without upsetting its stillness.

Like a Christmas ornament, the cauldron shattered revealing a crystal mask flickering with light. With the cauldron's pieces washed away, a drenched naked body of man in a fetal position remained. The mask hovered above him. He grabbed it and, together, he and it fragmented into a pile of small glass shards. The glass floated about like dust flakes and crumbled a thousand more times into a fine powder that then took on a shape of a young boy. A drop of honey fell from some void above, marked the boy's head, and he took in his first breath. Life coursed through his eyes. A majestic hill rose before him and a splendid city rose atop the mound. The city and the hill burst into the most intense hellfire, but the flames didn't burn long as great dragon wings burst forth from within the mound and became an imposing wave of water that quenched the blaze's thirst.

Water rushed past me in a great torrent and the two figures stood tall against it, their hands firm on my shoulders. The boy and the wave disappear into the darkness, leaving only the hill behind. From within this solid night emerged a creature so devilish-looking that it stopped one's heartbeat to gaze upon it. My hands began to tremble. My breath stopped dead in my throat. Tears ran down my cheeks like rivers. I watched evil itself take temporal form: as dark as darkness itself, its hide shaggy and slick, it stood on two hooved legs, a demonic goat head sat atop its broad shoulders. Two enormous ram horns curved back behind its ears. The horns were ridged, yet slick, almost wet. It was neither beats nor man. It's face smiling, ever shifting. It noticed me and a serpent's tongue flickered from its amused lips. "Cyn'ryth," it said with a sneer.

Evil walked up to me and took my chin in its soft black hands. It looked at the figures beside me and in a benevolent voice spoke, "Past, present, and future: lesser evils you are showing him, knowing full well that he will open doors to greater ones." It paused and contemplated my eyes. "From the wasteland to the gallows you shall walk and condemn innocent blood to terror. The Eye has chosen well." It let go of my chin and walked off growing large and immense like a boundless shadow. "Nightmares, no matter how horrid, are still only dreams, and every dream must end the same: with waking eyes shuddering in gloom," it said and with one hoof smashed the hill.

A bright light surged up the creature's body. It screamed in agony and exploded into a thousand pieces of darkness. Like fog, the pieces dissipated forming the crystal mask from before. The mask spun slowly before me and reflected all of time like a mirror. I saw everything for a moment, but it overwhelmed my senses and I retched out time itself. A gecko with clocks for eyes crawled out of the ground and licked up the puddle of time. "You humans, always wasting time," it scolded me, and just as it crawled out, it crawled back into the ground. Instantly, the mask and I were separated by a chasm of time.

Three animals materialized below the mask: an armadillo, a toucan, and a snapping turtle. The animals shriveled and withered away into singular points before burgeoning into a pocket watch with thirteen hands, a syringe with a luminescent liquid inside it, and an ornamental golden dagger. The mask boiled and melted away to form a noseless man with eyes on the brink of tears. He held his arms above his head and the items circled around him. Another man, this one made of light, appeared before him. Upon taking shape, the syringe flew at him, stabs into his abdomen, and he becomes flesh. The hands of the pocket watch spun faster and faster still. The once-luminescent-man's movements slowed to a crawl. As fear and shock spread across his face, an evil smirk curled up on noseless man's. He took the blade and stabbed him. Suddenly, a tall peak grew from below their feet and they stand atop its summit. Clouds whisked past them. One man smiled, one man wailed, and below them men with guns fought, fell, and died screaming for their mothers.

The dying men became worms and slithered over one another in pools of slime. Those soldiers who remained human froze like statues. Hate, fear, anger, and sorrow solidified upon their brows. Their bodies hardened into porcelain with multicolored quartz spiking outwards from their eyes, heart, and palms. Moved into rows by an invisible hand, the statues reminded me of the legend of the lost Qin Shi Huang's Terracotta Army. The figurines stood still for a long time: dirt and grime accumulated over them. A light shined from above and a group of gnomes, a black boy, and a wolfdog made of starlight appeared before the frozen army. The gnomes, statues, and wolfdog melted together and formed the man with the sown lips. The man acknowledged me with a nod and flew off into the sky leaving the black boy weeping and alone on the floor. The boy tore at his eyes then became one with the ground.

A blast of voices joined the blaring of an orchestra: a wonderful and frightening noise of the most chilling cantata. *Carmina Burana*. As the harmony awoke courage, resilience, and strength in one's heart, a one-armed man battled a wave of armor-clad warriors. One by one, he slew the scourge. One by one, his blade tasted blood and anguish. With his enemies defeated, he fell to his knees, the orchestra faded, the chorus did too, and out of the man's stump sprang a tree that consumed his body. He became it and it became him.

Like weeds, numerous Men sprang from the earth and surrounded the wondrous tree. Their hands became axes and they began to hack at the tree's mighty trunk. A great face of agony appeared on its bark and gave off a chilling shriek. Like tinder, the Men burst into flames. They smoldered; among their charred remains lay a woman. Humming a lullaby, she lovingly caressed her belly. As the flames faded she gave birth to twins: a boy and a girl. While an imposing moth swooped from the sky, an enormous earwig emerged from the earth. Together they stole the children away to the opposite ends of the world. The woman fainted, faded, and ended. The world was quiet. No wind, no distant noises beyond the horizon, only the sort of silence that makes men go mad from its stillness.

The two figures griped my shoulders. I looked up at them; tears streamed from their eyes. Their faces grew determined and menacing. I looked back to what unfolded in the near distance.

I saw the span of the life of the two children simultaneously: the girl become a woman and stood mighty and resilient against a great bull whose head reached the sky; meanwhile, the boy grew into a man and stood before a spider-like old man with three featureless heads. The bull fell before the girl and the three-headed man fell before the boy. A rumble, like that of a crag breaking off from a mountain, echoed through the world.

The sky shattered and fell to the Earth in giant swaths of glass and dirt. Nothing remained but rubble. The Dream became a Nightmare. A strange man and an odd girl fell atop the heap of shattered sky. The man looked on the ruined world with a sneer, the girl wept. The two become one with dual faces upon a single head. Their one body began to fight itself and tear at its own flesh until wounded, bloody, and torn—exhausted—it fell to the ground. From under the rubble came a rumbling, the mirror mask emerged from the ruined world and the One Body touched it. The mask shattered into an infinite number of pieces that then flew off into the broad world.

The One Body split into two: the boy and the girl who once stood before the bull and the three-headed man. The children noticed one another and reached out their hands toward each other but before they could touch, the boy fell through the debris into Hell where he met the Three-faced Traitor. Like Dante before him, the boy climbed out from the infernal pit. When he emerged, the girl had become a woman, not the one whom stood before the bull, but the one with living butterflies on her flesh. The woman spoke to four large creatures: an elephant, an octopus, a dragon, and a vulture. The animals nodded at one another, then placed their limbs onto the woman's head. "I'm sorry," she said to them, the beasts understood then exploded into orbs of ash.

The man with the sown lips descended from the shattered sky while a great number of figures emerged from the earth. An endless field stretched out before them and when Sown Lips landed, they battle him. However, he was much too powerful for them to handle. He obliterated most of his challengers. So much blood was spilled that the field became a scarlet sea. The boy fought hard, he fought bravely, and when an opportunity presented itself, he stabbed Sown Lips with the same golden blade that the noseless man once used. The world shook and a great shadow spread over the cemetery that was Earth. A sun-sized sphere of naked human bodies crawling over one another hung in the shattered sky. All of existence became an endless lament.

The remaining characters realize they had strings attached to their limbs. Strings that went up into the sky. They were all puppets to the Great Wolf, who in turn was a puppet to a beautiful woman and a handsome man—the same man and woman who stood beside me with their hands on my shoulders. The lamentation became deafening and my ears rung with agony. An immense White Door grew out of the scarlet sea and everything merged with it. Freud's words ricocheted in my head, "*Geseres* is a genuine Hebrew word derived from the verb *goiser*, and may best be rendered by "ordained suffering, fated disaster." From its use in the Jewish jargon one might think it signified "wailing and lamentation."[32] I saw the fate of everything: an endless lament of innocence, a harmony of dissonance, an aria of sorrow, a rondo of ruin.

The man and woman let go of my shoulders and I fell through the ground to, like a fish in water, float about in endlessness. I watched the stars and ran with them. Swirling blackness comforted me and I felt at ease with being. In the form of powdered charcoal, existential dread drifted out of me through my pupils.

32 Freud, 350.

The images of my past glittered in the charcoal flakes. The stars showed me a phantasmagoria of horror and mystery, of time. The beautiful woman and handsome man hovered above me. Their skin fell off like that of a porcelain doll. Hidden underneath were a thousand eyes, budding and crawling like ants over one another. They stopped their insectile paths and pierced me with their gaze. I felt an intensity of being watched by something ethereal.

"Do not let the future disturb you. You will meet it whether you want to or not. In hand, you will have the same tools you have now: your wit and your will, and perhaps some luck," it whispered. A pleasant melody sounded off in the distance then everything became blackness.

When I came to, I found myself in a ruin. My host's home lay decrepit and in disarray. The eastern wall had collapsed to form a mound of debris. The northern wall sat firm: nothing but black brick, no sign of a door ever set within it. Slightly dazed, I stood up. Crudely painted eyes within three halos covered the walls. I stood covered in a film of dust and cobwebs. My journal lay under some rotted wooden remains of a table.

A heavy black door sat on the western wall. I heard an indescribable echo in my head followed by something squeaking beyond the door. I pulled it open and entered a dimly lit room. Light came through the holes in the ceiling. The room lay clothed in complete wretchedness. The mummified bodies of my hosts lay in the bed in the middle of the room. Beside the bed and the path leading up to it, long-smothered black candles hid most of the room.

Cautiously, I walked up to the bed and, for a long while, stared upon their strange husks. In the middle of what once were their chests, sat two identical fleshy flowers; a film of slime covered the face-like pistil. The ugliness of the ghastly thing enchanted me. I took a step toward it to observe how the face—if I can call it that—moved and breathe. Shilling-sized bruises covered the fleshy petals. What looked like a pillow of belly fat acted as a sepal.

Suddenly, the flower gave off a cry of a small child in distress. I've had enough. The whole situation was too much for me to comprehend and, wanting to I understand none of it, I fled. I grabbed my journal and rushed outside. It was a ghost town, completely abandoned: some building lay crumbling, others had collapsed completely, others still sat half-covered by black sand and, like some unearthed archeological sites, stuck out of the dunes. White paint on black walls, an eye within three halos, covered every structure. The town was silent. Only the wind echoed among the ruins. I rushed across town, past the collapsed arch, past the sand-engulfed well, and toward the stables. Along the way, I ran into a haggard woman and rag-draped child.

The two of them surprised me as much as I did them. We stared at each other for a long minute. The woman looked like Donatello's *Penitent Magdalene*,[33] emaciated and estranged. The child's oil-smeared face was missing a left eye. They held some rusted pots and scraps of weatherworn material. Scavengers of some sort, I assumed. I took a step toward them and the woman dropped what she held to shield the child from who she presumed was a threat.

"I'm not going to hurt you," I said and showed her my palms. "What happened here?" I motioned to the village. Holding the child, the woman stepped back. To ease her fears, I too stepped back. Seeing this gesture, she pointed to the haloed eye, and in an insectoid voice—which I oddly understood—she said, "The Eye of Eyes took them away long ago. When the Legion came."

"But yesterday—"

"There lies a curse upon this land," she said. "The eyes are a

33 A realistic wooden sculpture from the Italian Renaissance depicting a gaunt Mary Magdalen.

warning. A sinister terror comes here in the night. Long ago and far away, a deranged woman wanted a child, but she couldn't have it, so she went from town to town and killed the children. Like a grim reaper, she wandered the Plane and came upon this here town when the Eye came. Her malice enchanted the Eye, so it gave her what she wanted. She gave birth to horrors and still does. Forever, until the Legion doesn't need her to anymore. She wanders from ruin to ruin feeding on the remnants of the memories of abandoned towns. You see, she's trying to escape the Eye. Escape her fate: to give birth to the servants of the Legion against her will."

A horrid scream pierced the air. Not waiting to see what gave off the shriek, the woman and child fled. I too was in no mood to find out, so I ran to the stables. They had fallen into greater ruin than before. Like the flaps of a box, the walls have fallen to the outside while the roof sat shattered on the near hillside. My aerocraft sat unharmed in the middle of this wreck. I ran to the craft, but stopped twenty yards out. Children's bones and skulls littered the ground while four large heaps of malformed bones and skulls lay where once the four corners of the stables sat. I rubbed my eyes with amazement. None of this was here mere moments ago.

With my mouth ajar, I got into the craft, quickly turned the heat and all measuring devices on, and prepared the balloon for takeoff. It took no longer than half an hour to get everything ready. Thankfully, the dread I felt made for decent fuel to get me working quickly.

As the craft neared readiness, I noticed movement near the shattered roof: a person lay half-covered by debris. My gut feeling told me not to go, but I ignoring it, and went anyway. To my horror, there she lay, the woman from last night. She wasn't as dry or decomposed as the husband and wife, but she wasn't completely human either.

Juices oozed from her flesh. The only part of her that seemed alive were her terror-stricken eyes; they begged me for death. She slowly lifter her arm towards me. She was topless. Her skin, her breasts looked like shriveled fruit left under the summer sun. She took in a deep breath, her ribs gave off a loud crunch, her sternum split open between the breasts and a gigantic fleshy flower burst forth.

She gurgled and a thick yellowish discharge foamed out of her mouth and nose. I watched as the flower developed at a rapid pace: a face emerged from its pistil and instead of leaves there were half-developed fingers, toes, knees, and random portions of arms and legs. Patches of hair grew sporadically, here and there. The woman reached for me and in a frightened gurgle spoke, "They are you and you are them."

I chose not to stay. It was time for me to leave.

VI

THE AERO-CRAFT LIFTED off. A sense of joy surged through me, my friend. I was finally back on course, back to the journey. I hoped that I left the nightmare below. How wrong I was, how naïve. Every journey has but one outcome: it must end, but imagine a journey so bizarre, so twisted, so macabre that it continues without end. Repeating everything over and over and over. Forgetting, and repeating it again, ad nauseam. Imagine a life like that: endless. Only the young and ignorant see pleasure in eternity. Not I, not now. If I knew, I'd dive head first from atop the craft. My death would be a release. My end, a pleasure. But I didn't know what the suicide out at sea knew. I'd like to end it now, but I can't. They are out there and I must get them, I must stop them. There too many I's running about plotting wicked deeds. Too many selves with sinister motives. If I come knocking on your chamber door, don't trust me, my friend. Don't trust me!

[Jan Cichy's pencil-drawn self-portrait takes up the next page. It is posed as a half-body bust. Half of his face in human, the other side is twisted and malformed: a mix between a plant, insect, and a decomposing fungus. Below, written in pencil, is a quote from Fyodor Dostoyevsky's *The Double*, "The door from the next room suddenly opened with a timid, quiet creak, as if thus announcing the entrance of a very insignificant person…"][34]

As the craft rose, I heard the sea beyond the dune. I turned and watched, awaiting to see what lay beyond the bulge. However, just as the top of the dune came into view, the dune itself grew larger and taller. Like a concerned parent passing a homeless drunk, it did not wish for me to see. It barred me from seeing beyond it. The mound became a mountain, and the mountain became something new entirely: a great stone wall that soared into the sky and disappeared beyond the cloud tops.

The entirety of the wester horizon was blocked from view. To the north, I saw nothing but the Black Plane. Far off in the distance, at the horizon line, I think I saw what looked like a bull. By the size of it, and the distance separating it from me, the creature must have been enormous, as colossal as a continent-wide mountain range, its legs great towers of flesh. Even now, I'm not sure if what I saw was part of some delusional dream or what the Eye of Eyes had showed me. The Black Plane stretched to the east and south. Hillsides and shrubs sparsely populated the whole thing. What looked like black dust devils spun about in the east. I headed south along what had become the western wall.

The wall became less stone-like and took on an obsidian glimmer of the night. Occasionally, a gnarled tree grew out from its solid blackness. Certain spots resembled water rippling through a still pool. Eyes formed sporadically throughout its surface, but faded back into the blackness as soon as the craft passed by. In other spots, the wall was as reflective as a mirror, yet when I flew by it, instead of seeing the craft and myself, an odd fleshy bulbous thing stared back. It resembled a deformed anglerfish with insectile

34 1846 Russian novel about a man seeing his double in Tsarist-Era Saint Petersburg.

branches hanging from its belly, and where I stood, stood a prawn-like entity with an eye-engulfed head.

After what seemed like several hours of flight, strange things came into view that are difficult to describe without sounding insane. There were towns, yes, but they weren't built in accordance to reason. Chaos seemed to be the rule in its architectural design. No concentric layouts, no grids, no nuclei, no linearity. They were all amoebauesq. *Chaos carolinensis* of city planning. There were buildings, yes, but they were not of wood, glass, or stone, but of people, not corpses, but living, breathing men and women. Umbrella-like spires with ever moving grooves akin to channels found on water-smoothed stones found in dried up riverbeds. Buildings that rejected the laws of physics: weeping willow-looking structures that moved with the breeze. These things can only be described in terms of sentiments and contrasts because reasonably they were unreasonable.

[Backwards and reverse starts.]

I felt that nauseating sensation one gets when standing on a ship lulled by waves. That simultaneous comfort and anxiety. The strange feeling of excitement and unease atop a roller coaster that is about to drop. You know the feeling, the one right after the climb of the cart but just before the fall. That still restlessness. That same feeling you get before the first kiss with someone you like; the moment right before the act, the instant that the decision is made to embrace, that void emotion. It coursed through me and grew in intensity the deeper into this bizzaro landscape I flew.

The flesh architecture of strange unnatural angles that curved inwards terrified me. Bordering on the edge of collapse, twisting towers swayed back and forth. Bodies gripping bodies. Floors-worth of strained hands gripping at naked flesh while clothed men and women meandered the streets, alleys, and boulevards below. A woman stared out at me through the window of her flesh home. Her eyes were hollow. Her flesh stretched over her frame as if she wore an ill-fitted dress. She had hands on hands. Fingers on fingers. Palms on palms. Upon seeing me, distress poured out of her. In turn, my body trembled. These people lived in homes built of living, breathing people! I flew through the Abyss, through Tartarus, through Mictlan, through Naraka, and, any moment now, I expected to see Yama.[35]

An aura of morbidity and death hung over the city. I felt a dull shock reminiscent of learning that a loved one had died. The surreal emotion of an out-of-body experience where your mind tastes vertigo while your body undergoes a sense chill. Loneliness stuck to me like evergreen sap. I thought of death and what it meant to fade away from the world. After you die, others are in control of the image of who you were. Some make you out to be a monster, others a saint. The truth lies somewhere in-between. The memory of who you were is determined by the living. What a terrifying thought. The dead have no voice. They can't speak up for themselves, all they can do is listen and silently brood from their tombs. Death is as much a disappointment as life. While in life you were disappointed with your choices or the lack thereof, in death you are disappointed with your inaction, your inability to influence. Below, I saw both the living living inside the dead, and the dead housing the living.

Flesh towns gave rise to an expansive city of human-bound structures. Encased in a massive web-like dome composed of ooze-covered bodies, great skyscrapers of flesh reached toward void heavens. As I flew by, these men and woman reached toward me, their moans filled the air, their eyes hungered to add me to their collective configuration. These miserable masses were as much cerebral edifices as they were physical. They moved collectively as one, as a legion does. My friend, if you only saw this twisted city

35 Various version of the underworld from different religions. Yama: Hindu and Buddhist deity of death.

of forms: of all human potential wasted away and erected into infrastructure, into buildings, roads, canals, halls, homes, you'd tremble from the implication. These living bricks, these wasted futures, made up everything.

[Backwards and reverse ends.]

I knew not how long I've flown above this City of Flesh, because I could not look away from it: from its twisted architecture of nonsensical design, inwardly curves, globules of flesh, giant orbs of Men holding great mirrors, and towers twisting in on themselves like seaweed in the deep, swaying back and forth. Buildings caressing buildings, flesh touching flesh. Their moans alone fashioned a waft. The city was alive and, literarily, breathing.

The madness receded into the horizon and again nothing before me but the black waste, nothing but a void in the land: no forests, no rivers, no lakes, just an endless expanse of earth. As before, time simultaneously sped up and slowed down. I flew at a crawl while the world around me became and ended and became again, until I saw nothing and everything in an instant. When time stabilized, I flew through an endless prairie of hanging men and women. Millions of them, noose-hung, as far as the horizon: a garden of the lynched and damned. Walking among them, like gardeners in an orchard, towering faceless giants clothed in black robes with immense hoods carried huge watering cans of bone. Blood flowed from their round spouts. The hanging masses squirmed below, their ravenous mouths open and hopeful for some crimson to quench their thirst.

Leafless trees, whose branches were nooses, hung heavy with the sins and repentances of their fruit. Watering their flesh harvest, the giants ignored everything that did not concern the Hanging Garden. The parched fruit lamented their thirst with wails of dismay. As the crimson fell from the spouts, each tree lifted its fruit skywards. The fruits raised their arms in an attempt to catch some liquid on their hand. Those that did, quickly licked at their hands and limbs. It was all a desperate sight that made my teeth rattle. Tears streamed down my cheeks when I caught glimpse of a fruit no older than ten desperately swiping at the scarlet rain. The writings of Hegel and Marx meandered through my mind. What I saw below stood as an allegory for the reality of working men and women who, like those hanging masses, reach out their hands to their employer overlords begging for a bite, for a chance at survival in the trenches of existence. These endless herds breed indefinitely not to pass on their genes or memories or traditions, but to bathe in the struggles of today. To exist is to pretend at a happy ending.

The withering worms crawling out from the dark earth to bathe in the warm rains, to become prey to the feathered predators above, this was Man, this is who he's always been. The tragedy of his presence is that he entered this play of existence with only a few minutes left until curtain call, and even though he wasn't there when the world formed, when it burned and drowned, when one plague, one disaster, one after the other, fed on what flesh there existed—be it reptilian, mammalian or otherwise—he still complains of his own small sorrows. And why shouldn't he? All he knows is the torments that other Men inflicted upon him, and what God deems his anguish—his life—is accepted as his fate, his punishment, his lot.

What I saw below was what existence truly is: humanity struggling to make sense of life through this feeble, yet adaptable form that it calls *the body*. From the numerous daily emotions coursing through it to the precise prowess of its reason, everything from the depth of the oceans to the heights of starlight, all of it is perceived through the membrane of flesh. But to what end? To pass on to our offspring what little grains of knowledge we had gathered as a species? To give our children, their lives a better shot at finding true beauty, true goodness, real pleasure, real love, all the good and righteous things in the world? To make men and women out of children?

No!

The answer is a grim paradox. We live and we breed so that the struggle can continue, so that the universe can feel, so that for every laugh there exist a dozen cries of anguish, for every one success a dozen failures, for every one will to action a dozen wills to inaction. Human life is an experiment in entropy and ennui. Our cities are hives of boredom, dullness, jealousy, and hunger. What you see in your neighborhood, your towns, villages, and homes, you see in individuals. And the hunger only grows vaster until one stands before himself and through the corrosion of his innocence, his morals, his resolve, that which he experiences outside himself seeps into his insides, and it screams at him, "You are bad, greedy, a victimizer, an oppressor, a thief, a scoundrel, a demon, a devil, a beast! You are vile, punish yourself, suffer, die!" And so, he becomes what he *thinks* himself to be, what others have made him out to be. He becomes an imagined character, a fictional personality made tangible: he becomes a strawman—easily burned, easily doused, flimsy, held together with delicate string, ready to be blown away by the gentlest breeze.

My friend, I may have no faith in goodness and devotion, but think not that I'm unaware that, at least, through friendship and love we can endure! They are the glue of humanity! They bind our collective future to the past and sacrifices of our predecessors. When those things are taken away—I speak of goodness and love here—when what makes us different from the beasts, when that human element is pulverized in a pestle and mortar of malice and jealousy, does Man fall prey to the reptilian part of himself. Nachash (שָׁחָנ)[36] emerges and he feast, and he kills, and he hisses with joy. He smiles.

The human spine and skull are but the remnants of the serpent within us. Take away our arms, legs, and intellect and what's left is

---

36 A variant of the Hebrew name of the Serpent from the Garden of Eden.

a belly to slither upon. The reptilian nervous system accompanies us everywhere, it is a part of our mind and soul, and it wishes to return us to the past. We struggle so greatly against this primordial, void-hungry part of ourselves. Doom is what it wants. Death is what it yearns for. Obedience is what it demands. The serpent within us has a name and it is Cyn'Ryth; from it stem the mythological Tiamat, Leviathan, Hydra, Nachash, races of Nāga, Jörmungandr, Falak, Python, Grootslang, Xiangliu, Quetzalcoatl,[37] and the like. It demands sacrifice of the highest magnitude: kindness, reason, love, family, brotherhood, courage, wisdom, and above all else, freedom.

Return to the dirt. Crawl upon your belly. Kill with your teeth. Gnash upon the stones all that makes you stand. Become unwound, untethered from humanity. Return to the shadow. Crawl back into Plato's cavern[38] and watch the specters dance from within your hole. Be being unquestioned. Be false and unwise. Be obedient only to the Legion. Question nothing. Serve the light-seeking darkness that surrounds the stars. That is the only thing that Cyn'Ryth demands. Be, just not human.

You know what I mean, my friend? Of course, you do! Take a boat into the middle of a lake and look above you. What do you see? The sky, an infinite expanse that swells beyond you, beyond your flesh, your feelings, your reason, that is the depth of humanity: to discover, to be creative, to bask in the sunlight. To be in the infinite and borrow from it something to make our own. To experience and give. And when the time comes to return what you have taken—with those additions that were your own—you may be proud, and rest well in the dirt, knowing that future generations can borrow what you've returned and add themselves into it.

---

37 Various serpentine creatures from different mythologies.

38 Reference to the Greek philosopher's allegory where people see shadows on a cave wall believing them to be reality, and not an imitation of said reality.

Now turn toward the water and look below. What do you see? Murkiness, blackness, shadow. Unknown depths that demand a life of obedience. The below consumes. Above demands flight, it is difficult to achieve, but it queries for choice, for fate, for action and will. Below demands plummeting, it is easier, and asks nothing of the falling beside obedience and servitude: a complete surrender of the I to the fall. No struggle against ego, only submission. One does not grow great from obedience. Growth stems from a will to climb, to fly, to choose for yourself. Unfortunately, many choose to plummet. The fall is always easier than the climb.

These are the differences between the falling and the climbing man, between the sadness of fear and the will to challenge it. This field of hanging bodies spoke of those differences, spoke of the choice of the multitudes: surrender to inaction, obey the will of the serpent!

I heard the sea again. The western wall became a great swelling wave. All features of solidity disappeared from its surface. There was a mighty roar of a wave crashing upon the crags of a shore, then a million horses brayed from within the surge. Above me, the sky shook. In one singular drop, from every part of it, came down a great torrent of blackness. An ocean of shadow descended and swathed everything. The world faded. If it was perceivable through the five senses, it became bareness. All that was became the night above and the night below. Oblivion became existence.

Horace wrote, "I shall not die wholly for a great part of me will escape the grave."[39] I felt what he meant. It was not the first time during this strange journey that I have felt like a sliver of nothing, but during this erasure, I knew that I was truly beyond the physical scope. My soul was transferred elsewhere. The only way to describe it is that I felt only knowledge. I felt the tears of all my ancestors streaming down some metaphysical cheeks, I felt

39 Roman poet.

their laughter, their struggles, despairs, hopes, and even sins. A collective experience of my precursor surged through the vapor that was Jan Cichy.

It felt nice. It felt soothing. I felt like a water bead escaping a melting block of ice.

In a moment, perhaps in a lifetime—I'm not sure—everything within the near distance of me returned. As if painted anew upon a black canvas by an invisible hand, suspended in a void, I stood inside the aero-craft. A peaceful sensation washed over me; the same sort of feeling, I assumed, that comes over all on the verge of death. I felt light and blissful, and ready to fade into the nocturne. The end, I craved it.

Then the fuselage shook. A murmur came from the left side of the cockpit. I glanced over. Holding on to the netting was a less developed version of myself. It had my eyes, my form, my face, but it was slightly less me and slightly more *something* else. It was uncanny and vaguely malformed. Its eyes weren't eyes, but resembled them. No soul dwelled within them. The ears had no will to hear. They lacked an external auditory canal. Flesh sat where none should have. The nose and mouth were ornamental. I gasped. The thing sensed me, looked up, and gave off a symphony of insectile clicking. With its twisted, but not fully developed, hands it climbed toward me. I had no intention of keeping this stowaway on my craft.

I grabbed the nearest tank of helium and threw it at my double. The canister struck the creature on the forehead. The imposter slid down, but didn't let go of the netting. It gave off a sickly, phlegm-filled shriek that echoed through the darkness. Then I saw it!

It emerged from the gloom: an enormous eye within eyes with flaps of vaginal labia minor flesh around it like petals of a delicate flower. A profound yellow and scarlet light emanated from it. Where the yellow became scarlet sat a void. Not black, not white but an indescribable missing space where nothing existed:

not time, not space, only an abyss of boundlessness. Eye globules fled from the vacuum.

I gazed into it, and it gazed into me, past my flesh and into my soul. It freed me from reason and bestowed me true understanding. It blessed me with madness. It gave me truth.

[Frantic scribbles and illegible verses fill the next several pages.]

Sand below, sea waves behind me. I awoke on a beach. I later learned from the people who found me that I washed up on the Spanish shore. Torn open, the balloon lay ahead of me upon some jagged rocks. The aero-craft itself was lost to the ocean, or perhaps it's still floating somewhere in the void with the Eye. Wherever it is now, it's beyond the reach of Man.

Instinctively, I reached for Saint Christopher's medallion, but a torn necklace is all I grasped. The medallion was gone. A haunting feeling erupted from my abdomen. I felt horrible nausea and dread. But just as quickly as the feeling came, it sunk down into my depths. My innards knew: all was wrong with the world.

[Jan handwrote Cyprian Kamil Norwid's poem 'Do Not Call Me to a Humble Hymn' in-between what I delineated as sections six and seven. The two following pages include the original Polish version of the poem and my translated one.]

Ty Mnie Do Pieśni Pokornej Nie Wołaj
- Cyprian Kamil Norwid[40]

Ty mnie do pieśni pokornej nie wołaj,
Bo ta już we mnie bez głosu;
A jeśli milczę, nie przeto mnie połaj,
Kwiatów, Ty, nie chciej od kłosu.

Bo ja z przeklętych jestem tego świata,
Ja bywam dumny i hardy,
A miłość moja, Bracie, dwuskrzydlata:
Od uwielbienia do wzgardy.

Szkoda, mój Bracie, na wiatr ducha wywiać
I krew wypluwać tęsknotą,
Żeby siedzących w cyrku uszczęśliwiać,
Więc mów, że milczę tak oto.

Gdy w głębie serca purpurę okrutną
Wyrabia prządka cierpienia,
Smutni—lecz smutni, że aż Bogu smutno—
Królewskie mają milczenia.

---

40 An 1855 poem written by 19th century Polish Parnassianist poet and dramatist, Cyprian Kamil Norwid.

Do Not Call Me to a Humble Hymn

by Cyprian Kamil Norwid[41]

Do not call me to a humble hymn,
Because it is voiceless in me already;
And if I am silent, do not scold me,
Do not yearn for flowers from a thorn.

Because I am of the damned of this world,
I may be proud and arrogant,
As for my love, Brother, it is two-winged:
From adoration to contempt.

It is not worth, my Brother, to squander one's soul on the wind
And spit blood with longing,
To make happy sedentary circus audiences,
Thus speak, that I'm silent because.

When into the heart's depths a crimson cruelty
Bores via a teetotum of suffering,
The unhappy—but so unhappy that even God is dismayed—
Bear a Divine silence.

41 This translation is my own. It is not a literal translation, but a symbolic one focused on the poems intended, but also interpreted, meaning. Due to the difficulty of translating Norwid's metaphors and allegories, I chose to alter some phrases to convey its meaning into modern English. The original Polish version is included as a companion piece.

VII

MY JOURNEY BACK to England remains a hallucinogenic blur of distant faces, unidentifiable noises, and absent moments. What little I remember, I'll explain to you, my friend, because there must be a record of as many details of the horrors that followed my return to this Dream as possible.

Upon the Spanish beach, a couple approached me as I awoke. We communicated through what little we knew of each other's languages, before I rushed off. I had to, I fell into a blinding madness. I wasn't sure if all I saw was an illusion crated by the Eye or if I was, in fact, back on Earth. Men resembled phantoms, trees resembled ethereal tendrils, only the animals were themselves. I made my way to some village, I remember a mule, an old man and his buggy. How far he took me is beyond my recollection. I did make it to Valencia, then Zaragoza before getting on a boat in San Sebastián. Who I spoke with, how I paid my fare, or even where I slept is all lost to me. I recall filching food from markets and street stands. I recall begging for money in Zaragoza, and getting a proper beating from some rough *gendarme*. Perhaps, what I begged out of the Spaniards, I spent on the fare back to England. Perhaps, not. I have a dim memory of magnificent talking bird with heavenly plumage. It spoke of giving direction to the lost. It had a sweet voice, like how I imagine cherubs speak.

My next proper memory is of a man shouting and threatening to throw me overboard. "Enough with your prophesizing!" I remember him yelling. Then there was a commotion, a chase, some Bobbies[42] with malicious words, and I awoke in delirium on the floor of my flat. I spent the next couple of days' floor-bound. I didn't want to do anything, didn't want to move, eat, or breath. I slept, and when awake, I lay, as if dead, in some catatonic state. To my disgrace, I relieved myself where I lay. My mind felt like pulp, overexerted, drained, and incapable of comprehension.

[Backwards and reverse starts.]

After the initial asthenia ran its course, I spent hours soaking in the tub. My body recovered some of its basic utility to preserve itself. I even used soap to rid myself of the layers of bodily grime. The hours passed. Warm water grew cold. I didn't feel the change. I kept lying in my own filth. It wasn't until I had fallen asleep, and almost drowned in my own bathwater, that my mind attempted to grasp what it had experienced. Leaving the bath behind, I lay naked on the floor. Every turn became an impasse, every path a dead end. From where I had begun my journey to where I had finished it, nothing connected. What happened to me and the aero-craft was nonsensical. Nothing, and I mean nothing, made sense. I feared that I was insane, then I dawned on me, a Eureka! moment, that I was blessed because *I was insane*. Glory be to the Eye! I though. Glory be. My excitement quickly faded when I remembered my parents and the failure to circumnavigate.

Something deep down—perhaps shame, perhaps some prodigal son insecurity—forced me not to return to my parent's farm. I couldn't face them. Not like this: a failure in every respect. I wanted to apologize to them. But to do so meant that I'd have to admit aloud that I have become what they had feared most—what

42 British slang for police. Named after Sir Robert Peel who set up the first proper police force in the United Kingdom: The Metropolitan Police.

I feared most: their son was a disappointment. I wasn't ready for that.

While I failed to circumnavigate the globe, what little adventuring I did wasn't a complete waste of time. The Eye had revealed a grander experience to me, a grander world of metaphysical fissures between the real and the abstract. I discovered a plethora of, for a lack of a better word, Dreams. I saw the loops and lemniscates that molded everything. I saw the infrastructure of existence. From the paths of ants to the routes of galaxies, everything reverberated with repetitiveness, constancy, and uniformity. Originality is a lie, it is but a rediscovery of the motions that have been forgotten, or lost, or too silent for us to hear. There sits an infinity beyond humanity's societal traps. People going places they don't want to go, doing things they don't want to do, with people whom they don't like and have no connection to beside the bondage to some place, job or society, and why do they do this? Why do they jump into monotony so willingly and with such fervor? What is their reward for this endless tedium?

[Backwards and reverse ends.]

Men enter shops to buy things: a new jacket, some trousers, a purse, sparkling jewelry, latest cutlery. Like a circus ape, now they have something new to play with, to waste their time with until, yet again, they return to the same place, same job, to see the same people whom they find, at the least, annoying and dull. Life is the ability to create inabilities. This is existence: anxiety and shopping, constant outdoing and contrasting between a bunch of bovine cretins who have nothing but fucking, feeding, and freeloading on their mind.

Most Men exist in this revolution of monotony and they think this is life, this is all there is: a good job, a loving spouse, and unquestionable servitude and obedience to the job, to the state, to society, to this or that religion. Snap your fingers and, suddenly, Man becomes a heartless husk that identifies with only one thing: submission.

As a student, my soul knew that civilization and its pleasantries were a lie, but now all of me knows it. All of me feels it. "Peace and freedom," the rhetoric of the ruling and wealthy. Ha! "War and bondage," the actions of the ruling and wealthy. What they say is not what they do. How long must the common Man play dumb? Or perhaps he fears to know, fears to stand up? A kneeling Man must depend on others to feed him, an upright one can walk and chose his meal. Men have forgotten to walk. They believe they were born on their knees. They believe a pair of loafers and a walking stick are a ball and chain.

[The following page holds a sketch of a kneeling figure. Its head is split open. Stars, galaxies, and horrifying creatures are escaping the gash upon its brow. Below the image, written in pencil, sits a quote from Blaise Pascal's *Pensées*. It reads, "All things can be deadly to us, even the things made to serve us; as in nature walls can kill us, and stairs can kill us, if we do not walk cautiously."][43]

The Eye showed me all of time, and in so doing, it had awoken me to the reality that this Dream exists. When you're asleep and dreaming, my friend, you watch, like some heaven-hung angel, all that happens to your dream self. You are an observer in your own mirage. That is what the Eye does, that is its role: it watches you and me, and everyone, and everything all the time. Even now, as I write this and as you read it, it watches. I can sense its gaze dissecting every one of my thoughts and judging them on their worth.

The feeling is much the same as the one you get when reflecting on your parent's judgment of your own choices. Did I act justly? Did I act in accordance with what they wanted? Did I do them dishonor by my choices, by my actions? The pressure! The weight! It's too much. I feel now what Sisyphus must have felt with every climb and descent. With every disobedient stone. I

43 An unfinished collection of thoughts and reflections by mathematician and philosopher, Blaise Pascal.

know that if I return to them, to my parents, their eyes would fill with pity and regret, and their downcast glances would be the death of me. I cling to an illusion of self-worth because if I don't, disillusionment is bound to set in, and that would be hemlock to my ego, a death sentence to my future.

A noose and a beam. A blade and a warm bath. A bridge and single leap.

I hate them for it. I hate them for influencing my own self-suggestion. My God, what's left of me? Remorse, resentment, and madness? This I know: all children hate their parents and regret it. To hate one's creator is a human characteristic, one that differentiates us from the beasts. Contrarily, all parents—at least at some point or another—see their children as less than themselves. The creator knows that he can't make something akin to himself, it would mean existential suicide. One cannot make his creation better than, it would defeat the purpose of being the creator, the authority. A *better me*—in the form of the created—is a danger to the order imposed by the maker. This is the paradox of the child and parent, of God and Man, of the Eye and the Head in which it sits. There is always a struggle between parent and child, between experience and ideology, between expectations and innocence. Yet, the outcome is always the same: forward momentum, forgetting, and repetition. In a word, recurrence.

Freud wrote, "One evening, before going to bed I had disregarded the dictates of discretion not to satisfy my wants in the bedroom of my parents and in their presence, and in his reprimand for this delinquency my father made the remark: 'That boy will never amount to anything.' It must have terribly mortified my ambition, for allusions to this scene return again and again in my dreams, and are regularly coupled with enumerations of my accomplishments and successes, as though I wanted to say: 'You see, I have amounted to something after all."[44] The parents judge

44 Freud, 188.

and the children reject the judgment by challenging its conclusion. But sometimes the judgment is correct and the child becomes his destined self: a failure, an embarrassment, a loser. Because of this, I chose not to return to my parent's farm. If I returned there, I'd be hurting them, hurting myself and—while not aware of it at the time—putting them in danger. A couple of days into this reflection on my relationship with my parents, I felt as if I was being observed by more than just the Eye. The doubles were watching.

I got up off the floor. It must have been nearing a week since I've gotten back. Looking at myself in the mirror, an emaciated and unshaven man looked back. Since my return, I haven't eaten anything and drank only sink water. I didn't know what to do, so I momentarily returned to the monotony: I shaved, I dressed, I cleaned the flat. In other words, I did nothing of worth. Toward evening, I stepped outside to buy some bread and meat, and after eating, I sat at my table contemplating what to do next.

I couldn't involve my parents in the things I've seen. The old cannot understand the new, least of all, the chaotic, demonic, and ethereal newness. My friend, I knew that I could only trust you with this report. Why? Because you'll understand almost none of what I write. You're a rational and logical sort of fellow, a fellow who recognizes madness and superstition in the minds of common folk. You'll see clearly through the archetypes and peasant sensibilities that my mind has become. You understand the difference between science and magic, between the real and the fabricated. That is why writing to you, recording the madness within, is a reflection on and a rejection of my ordeals. I assume, as I must, that you'll dismiss everything that I've written, and attribute it to folly and delirium. Because of that, I know that you'll be safe from the tendrils that reach out from the twilight. You'll be clear of the coming corruption, because you'll be dead by the time it arrives.

['Ha! Ha! Ha!...,' written in red and black ink, occupies the following page.]

If I wrote to my parents, they'd worry about my well-being and fear for my current state of my mind. It's too late. I am madness. I am insanity. I am lunacy. I am Man. It had to be this way. Many write of Destiny as a self-chosen path, but that is wrong. Destiny is a labyrinth and, while yes, we chose what corners to turn and what straightaways to follow, in the end, we are moving through a labyrinth not of our own making. We reach a point that we call our Fate and congratulate or scold ourselves on the outcome. What a sad state of affairs this is, to believe that the end follows from our choices and not the alternatives decreed by the tendrils of time. Such is Man: he must believe that there is some control granted to his short-lived existence.

Having been blessed by the Eye, but doomed by my mitosis, I knew I could not stay in London. After tidying the flat, I did the only thing I could do: I emptied all my financial accounts, closed all memberships, canceled all newspaper and informational subscriptions, and paid an estate broker and an attorney to sell my flat and transfer all the funds from the sale to my parents. The same day, I signed all the proper paperwork and notarized a contract in which I stated that the monies from the sale must be sent to Snowshill in exactly thirteen days. I also packed several parcels—with my clothes, small furniture, and the like—and paid for a carrier to deliver the items to my parent's farm the following week. There was no need to return to the patent office. For what? To be bothered by question, perhaps even ridiculed for my failures? No, no, no. There was no need for that. Nor did I wish for any chance reunions with anyone I knew, especially, from that mediocrity factory.

I must admit, however, that contacting the estate broker, then the attorney, felt like a fitting challenge for a broken mind. These normal and proper men had no clue of the terrors beyond the organized reality they've been conditioned to accept during their lifetime. They knew not of the ever-consuming horror outside this

Dream: the blackness of the void, the silence in the abyss, the nothingness outside space.

"Well that's fine," the estate broker said, after I had explained my need to sell and what had to be done with the funds. "Well that's fine," the attorney parroted. I tried, I truly did, but I could not help myself. I burst into manic laughter. "Nothing is fine! Nothing ever will be!" He thought me a madman, of course, but such is life. Often, those aware of the truth are mocked and labeled as loonies. I promptly departed his office.

As of this writing, I know full well that my parents received both the monies and loot. I can, at the very least, know that I did that for them. What I couldn't provide in esteem and pride, I offered in currency and possessions.

I rid myself of any excess furniture and extravagances. There are plenty of scoundrels willing to pay for what I was selling. The currency went into my pocket as funds for the journey ahead. I stayed in some old harbor woman's day-to-day rental room for a few days. It was cheap and the woman, wisely, chose not to engage in conversation. Prompt daily payments is all she cared about. I spent the days planning my escape from this reality and concluded that the Continent was a good place to hide.

I felt it then. The chase. The sensation of being choked by an invisible enemy, a fire-drenched hand constricting my windpipe. I didn't know then, but there were numerous hands tearing at my throat. Numerous eyes observing, judging on how to handle me, how to attack and take away what little humanity I still had left. They desired to replace me. To consume me, not figuratively, but literally. The enemy hungered for my essence.

The double can only become the real thing when it owns the memories of that which it hopes to become. We do that. We all know someone who we envy, someone who's life we desire. Some of us choose to imitate, consume, and become the other. All the while, losing everything that makes us, us. Life is full of these little imitations: wearing your hair different, walking around in shoes you don't usually wear, using jargon instead of words that come to you naturally, carrying yourself like another, the shift in body language, etc.

It's the myth of Theseus' ship incarnate: are we still ourselves if every part of us is an imitation of someone else? The answer is no. We become the other pretending to be ourselves. That is why we trust people who dress like us, talk like us, act like us. The mass psychology of self-reflecting in others is the rule in society. My replicas knew this. They knew of the constant loss of self to the will of the mass. They wished to take, like the mass does, what little self of me that remained and make it their own. They knew that it was the only way to filch my immortality from me. Take Man's soul away from him and you take away all that makes him happy, sad, anxious, all that makes him human. Take the soul, leave the husk, leave the mechanical, submissive, and tame.

My friend, there are two immortalities: the minor one when you are remembered by those who knew you, and the major one when the *impression of you* is evoked by those whom you never met. After your death, the two play a game of tug-of-war: the real you battles the imagined you, the memories-blinded one. Take Fyodor Dostoyevsky as an example. He was a horrid man: gambler, philanderer, drunk, etc., and, yet, is remembered at a poet of the human soul, an intricate painter of the web that is the human condition. The two immortalities are a paradox. They present a Minotaur: human and beast, real and imagined, tranquil yet violent.

My doubles want both of my immortalities. They wish to smother me with oblivion.

If they steal the essence of who I am, then the I that people remember won't be me, but some other self, a creation of my replicas. The same can be said of the imitated I: the I we present to the world—this persona with its many masks and many coats—is in fact us in a state of fear. Fear of judgment. Fear of shame. Fear of neglect, loneliness, misinterpretation. We don't want to express ourselves to others as who we really are, because sometimes we're less than beasts. Sometimes we're monsters.

The doppelgängers know it. I know it. Because of this I had to flee London.

I made my way to the grocer to buy some provisions. Along the way, I bumped into one of my former colleagues from the patent office. The man was pleasant in that 'lifelong bureaucrat dealing with a customer' sort of way. "How is everything?" he asked without wanting the real answer. "Thankfully, it's getting warmer," he laughed at an observation he made. It was all manufactured. It was all false, like a *Caligo idomeneus*[45] pretending to be an owl: espousing appearances over substance. Insincere questions and mundane observations, the tools of an imitator.

I couldn't take it, this shallow man with his humdrum droning, mechanical responses that lacked the human spark. He spoke of the joy, of the privilege of working on this or that patent, of how the office atmosphere is like that or this, of how so-and-so is dealing with problem one or problem two, of how this client is not like the other, of how bonuses will be divided at the end of the quarter. In short, he spoke pure idle bullshit. And he didn't stop, oh no. His droning moved on to how he'd composed a new form for this and another for that. He took inhuman joy in explaining trash, because that is what it was, trash. His gibberish was my mind rubbish. Taking up space where more important matters should have been placed, analyzed, and kept. The universe didn't care what form was needed to claim a patent in field A over field B. If the dead didn't care, why should the living.

The longer he spoke of this bramble, the greater my rage grew

---

45 A South American specie of butterflies from the genus Caligo known for huge eyespots on their wings that resemble owls' eyes.

until—like a witches' brew in a cauldron—it had boiled over. I erupted, "You are a dull man who speaks only of his occupation! Whose whole being is based on, revolves around, and obeys the routine of that job. Do you think, that after you die, you'll be remembered for the work you did? For whether you filed this form or that form? For whether you stamped this sheet or that sheet? Stop this false equivalency. Self equals job? No. Self equals clothes? No. Self equals what others think of you? No. We are not the staples, tables, papers, or tasks assigned to us in our little cubicle. God damn it, be yourself!"

I fled from him. I could not stand that stupid face of his. I didn't buy any provisions, I went back to the room, packed what little I had, and hopped onto the first train out of town. I went to Ipswich, Norwich, Grimsby, Leeds, Manchester, Liverpool, Hereford, Bristol, and Portsmouth, stopping in several smaller towns along the way, sleeping where I could, eating what I was given. Fleeing.

I tried to shake myself of this ever-watchful Eye. It didn't take long to understood that you don't escape its gaze. Never. It's always watching, always teaching. I had to flee England, and break free from the mass of vermin who crawled upon their knees praising the Queen, the monarchy, the system of reliance as if it were God himself they praised. These masses, they are lost. They cherish thieves and tyrants over their own freedom. They cherish pageantry over their own intellect. *Panem et circenses.*[46] And what do they get from it? Nothing, but gossip to occupy their minds. Gossip so that they can pretend their lot is *better than*. Meanwhile, the monarchy laughs and collects, growing fat on the struggle of the corpus. What a repulsive society, and what a horrid ivy they had grown. A weed that twists and turns, that constricts, strangles and saps, that kills.

---

46 Latin for "bread and circuses." Quote is attributed to the Roman poet, Decimus Junius Juvenalis.

[Latin writing starts.]

It's all meaningless in the end, of course. The Eye had showed me. What humanity we built atop the ape skeleton—what elegance, from chewing on raw flesh to eating cooked meat—had been hijacked by the self-interest of the imitators, of the synthetic. Humanity is dying. Man is in hospice. As I write this, I am shaking at the thought of the eventual evaporation of every eye, of all the ways of perceiving the universe in all its cold glory. For that is our end, blind among the stars, hoping for some glimmer of light to warm our children by.

Eventually, from Portsmouth, I bought my way to the continent, but while awaiting a boat to across the Channel, I felt hunger and decided to buy something to fuel my emaciated self. I made my way off the port and entered a nearby shop, where I obtained bread and smoked sausage.

I left the shop and passed a local blacksmith—workshop and cart—who was selling his tools street-side. There I saw myself. Not in a mirror or the shop window, but before me, before my very flesh and blood, it stood, another me. It was dressed like a gentleman, and as far as I could see, its face was my own, as were its hands. This was not the deformed I from before—no! it was a functional other me. A true replica from before my emaciation.

I cannot properly convey the terror that I felt. To know that you are you, and yet, there before me stood all of me, all my experiences, memories, successes, and regrets. I and me in the street. Did him and I share all the things within me? Or did I share all the things with him? Who was the original and who was the copy? Who was the initial experiencer and who the imitator? I blinked, it blinked. I was terror-stricken, it smirked.

My hands shook.

A cold sweat spread across my brow. A panic overtook me that I had not felt since seeing the suicide plunge from my aero-craft. It was pure existential dread. I stood like a pillar. I was dumbfounded.

Somehow, I found a shred of courage and walked up to myself, or, perhaps, it walked up to me, I'm not sure anymore. It grabbed me by the shoulders and in my own voice it spoke, "Hollow eyes within the empty wolf skull watch life seep away, drank in by a shoal of lampreys that are the memories of who we once were. Blessed are the dead, for their flesh will never taste the star fire from above—from the tendrils of Cyn."

[Latin writing ends.]

I pushed the devil away, grabbed the nearest hammer from the hardware cart, and, with all my might, swung at my imitator. I missed. Not awaiting its reaction, hammer in hand, I fled down the street. Running blindly, I ended up in a labyrinth of alleyways. Left. Right. Left. Turning for turns sake. Every choice felt like an escape. Theseus fleeing the Minotaur. I ran to run, until Fate would have it, I ran right into myself.

This time I did not miss. I struck it right on the head, and as it fell, I hit it several more times: body and head, body and head. A perfumed madness, a saccharine rage, gripped me so that every blow of the hammer to its being felt like a sweet release, an ecstasy.

The rage passed, the madness lingered. I observed the twitching body, my body! A fleshy eye-covered flower with insectile legs flailed about in its gnashed head. It gave off a gurgling noise, stopped flailing all together, and receded into the wound like a deflated balloon.

I dropped the hammer and leaned against the nearest wall. Tears ran down my cheeks. Then I saw it. Off in the distance, another I watched. Another I…

I just stood there.

I fled.

VIII

I'VE BEEN ON the run for over a month. I'm exhausted. My mind is not my own. My body has escaped me, but it will not get far. I'm hunting it and I will continue to hunt it, until I've killed all of it. It must not take me. I am the first. If it takes me then it will know that it can do so to others, to all. It will consume and impersonate and breed. I won't allow it! I must cling to the hope that I can stop it. God! Existence is a curse, a torture.

I cannot tell you where I am. No one can know. Not you. Not them. Not it. Especially, it. I've killed three more of them. The only thing left for me now is to make sure I kill the rest. There aren't many left. I feel weaker with each kill. I think you know what that implies. These imitations are getting slyer after every hunt. They learn with every slaying. They observe my method, my approach, my strike, my strategy. One attacked me. It had so much strength. I felt as if I fought a bull in a Jan Cichy costume. My flesh was its attire. It was tough but I came out victorious. I…

[The writing on the next page is smeared. The page is wrinkled and water damaged.]

You'd never recognize me, my friend. As I've mentioned, I've grown weaker and weaker with each kill. I'm almost a skeleton. Nothing but skin and bones. Tendons stretched tight in my arms. The other day, I gathered courage to look in the mirror. My cheekbones poke out like jagged monoliths upon a bare landscaped.

My eyes have sunken deep into my skull. Pits of despair. There are no lips, just a vague sliver of thin crusted flesh. What little hair remains is gray and wispy. Brittle straw upon a steppe. My neck is ligaments, thin snakes constricting nothing but frail bone. I resemble a wraith. In forty years, Europe will be nothing but wraiths.

A child ran away from me in the street the other day. It saw Death. It fled. Perhaps, Siddhartha Gautama[47] too saw Death, before escaping under the Bo Tree. Perhaps, it was a vagrant. I cannot sleep and spend my wakefulness watching the sky, or the market with its people. The crowds lull me, their meandering, constant going and leaving. Where are they heading, and why? The constant rushing. "Hurry slowly," my grandmother used to say. Now she lies still under some earth beside some hedges. I think of her often just before catching a few minutes of slumber here and there. It doesn't last long—the respite—because even the smallest and faintest noise wakes me and I spring to my feet, knife at the ready.

The replicas, they want their vengeance. I know it. I've killed four of them. I stomped the last one's head in with my boot, and didn't stop until there remained only pulp and stain. I'm not sure how many are left, but there can't be more than two or three. I can feel it. Whatever happed beyond this Dream—at that damned village—these things are now connected to my essence, my life force. Suicide would solve everything. But what if it doesn't? A leech doesn't die with its host. It just moves on to another meal, another victim. The leech is a crafty parasite. They too have become crafty. One slipped a noose around my neck while I dozed. It pulled and I rose. Thank God for the poor constructions here. The beam broke. The roof feel. Now one of them is missing an arm.

That moment had taught me to move daily and never stay in

47 Buddha.

the same place twice. Unfortunately, they've been scouting potential locations of where I may appear next. "Hello again," a man whom I never seen before greeted me. He said he remembered me from the time when I stayed at his roadhouse the previous week. He noted I've grown lean. I fled. I just arrived at that town, there was no way this stranger would have known my face.

Prey hunting the predator.

They appear in crowded areas now, my friend. They know that it's safe. They assume it, of course. But if a chance presents itself, I don't care, I'll slaughter them before a crowd. Cut off their heads before an audience. They want to consume me. My flesh is in their way. The only thing they want is to eliminate me, then they can exist out in the world unimpeded. Why? I don't know. What reason there is for this pursuit is lost to me. Perhaps, like a tarantula hawk wasp, they lay their eggs within a worthy predator and wait for their offspring to burst forth? Perhaps, my memories are what their after? Perhaps, this is all just a game of cat and mouse, an entertainment? A torture? A penance?

The last one that I killed bit me. It wasn't good. My mind became clouded like when one has too much to drink. For the first couple of days, everything spun like in a whirlwind. Then the world became different. Only the Eye's revelations could compare. Men, women, animals and plants, even insects, all resembled gelatinous strands. All double-helix and cells. It was vexing to see everything as it is: a composition of chemicals and elements. For as rotten as I felt, the bite was a blessing. It made me perceive the world as the doubles do: structured chaos with each being as same as the other. They didn't see variation, eccentricity, beauty. Only sameness.

Small delineations make us different, make us individuals. But to live like that, to see the world as a set of chemical compounds, it kills the soul. It slays emotion and deteriorates humanity. It is perhaps why doctors and scientists are so cold, so mechanical, and, just like most engineers, they care only about the structure, and only the structure, and everything else is irrelevant. That is how Man will end the world: through immoral intelligence. He will see something that will be scientifically impressive and seductive, but morally and spiritually abhorrent. And instead of doing the difficult thing—shutting one's eyes and walking away—he'll pursue the scientific, he'll pursue ruin.

The White Door will open. It lies open now, beyond time, beyond space.

Man will grab the atom. He will embrace the mechanical. He will amalgamate himself with the synthetic leaving behind what makes him human for something colder, more practical, more supercilious. He will become a hull of a rotten ship, empty and reminiscent on what he once was: glorious sails, a mermaid at its prow, of the valor he once displayed against the mighty waves of existence. This cold Man will lie to himself thinking that he is better now, better in this weakened and sickly state of impersonality, because at least now he's achieved science, he's achieved synthetic godhood.

Man will sacrifice his immortality for the ability to say, "I told you so." What a whimper that will be: Man, the God-made, undone by intelligence. That is what these imitations are: pure intellect with no humanity, no emotion, passion, or rage. They do not understand laughter or the whistling of a jolly tune. They, like some praying mantis, know only patience before the strike, and judgmental condemnation of their prey. I cannot let them consume me! Never!

When the madness of this *methodological vision* lifted, I found myself in some slum. Where I bit myself, the flesh become gelatinous, like that of a jelly fish. It became a membrane of nothingness. Not flesh but slime. Not Man but sludge. Not life but septic rot.

I scorched a blade and cut out that part of my forearm where the flesh had become viscous. The next few days were spent in delirium: the images that the Eye had shown me intermixed with my childhood memories. I played fetch with my childhood Vizsla,[48] Reki, but it had no head, only a single large bloodshot eye. Next thing I knew, I stood in the woods picking mushrooms, only what I thought were portabellas, porcinis, or slippery jacks,[49] were malformed human fetuses. I lay in a field of crocuses that screamed in agony. Their souls were in inferno, while their bodies swayed in the green fields. Such horrors replayed in my head for days. Eventually, I healed and escaped onwards, into the depth of the Eurasian landmass.

As mentioned earlier, I'm sending this record to you, my friend, to my collegial home of Kraków, in the now Austro–Hungarian Empire, as an attempt at justify my actions between the aero-craft's launch and today. Rumors will spread. They must be dismissed as gossip and exaggeration. They are false. What I write to you is the truth. These are the facts. Someone must know of this lunacy, someone who is just close enough to me that knows that I am not entirely a madman. You are that man! You're in no danger, only I know of you. These false I's are oblivious to my youth, to our friendship. Their interest lies only in the immediate.

I've contemplated a return to the Continent, but to do so would take me back through Istanbul. I've had a dreary experience there. I cannot return through the Bosporus.[50] It would be the death of me, of that I'm sure. I killed myself there, but before I did, it had killed a bystander. To commit murder upon myself while I slew an innocent was a terrible ordeal. I'm a wanted man for a crime of a different self. Thus, the Continent is not safe for me. Only the Arabian Desert can benefit me in my slaying of these things. These secluded sands are my allies.

48 A Hungarian pointing and sporting dog breed. From Hungarian, meaning 'searcher.'

49 Types of edible mushrooms.

50 A narrow straight that connects the Black Sea with the Sea of Marmara.

The imposters know this, of course. They know that Arabia is a harsh land of warriors. They aren't used to this heat, to this constant exhaustion, to the life thief that is the desert Sun. Over the past few days, they've kept their distance. They are biding their time. They are adjusting to the new arena of our little game. They've begun wearing local attire. The other day, in the market, I followed myself but when I confronted me, I fled. I followed, thinking I can strike myself down. Another I down. Another I dead, but it wasn't so. I am often more competent than myself.

I led myself into a mosque only to lost track of me. But I didn't leave empty handed. Oh no. I came away with a sliver of knowledge. I saw all of me that remained: three more I's left, three more casualties. Then all that I brought back with myself can vanish. I can end. The curse, the knowledge, granted to me by the Eye can fade. It is the only way. I cannot live with the constant gaze of the Eye upon me. The gaze is ubiquitous. Every eye of every creature is its eye, and it sees, it knows what I'm doing.

I know what I did.

Their eyes—the imitation's eyes—are its eyes, too. They see. They see.

[The following page contains the phrase *Natura non constristatur*[51] in its center, with pencil drawings of various calamities around it: fire, flood, earthquake, war, etc. Just below the phrase, drawn in intricate detail, sits Michelangelo's *Pietà*.[52]]

You know, my friend, knowing what will be, does not give Man the tools of knowing how to stop it. If tomorrow the Eye of Eyes granted you the knowledge of the future, of all the good and all the bad that is to come, how would you react? Would you try to stop the bad? How? Where would you begin? Right now, millions are starving in British India. Can you save them?

51 Latin for 'Nature is not saddened.'

52 Famous sculpture depicting the body of Jesus Christ on the lap of his mother, Mary, after the Crucifixion.

No.

A volcano explodes, a tsunami rises, a disease spreads. You know this, but what can you do? Nothing. You can only watch silently, and attempt what you may to dodge destiny. The future is inevitable. It comes like a glacier upon a silent wood. At first slowly, but the next thing you know, the ice had ground the forest into splinters, leaving the earth flattened below its mighty mass. Events will happen that no Almighty can stop. People will be born, they will die, and the White Door, with or without your permission, will open.

Can a blade of grass stop a forest fire? Can a leaf stop autumn from arriving? Can one drop of water quench the thirst of a drought? Our role in this Dream is much the same. We can only observe, and change what we can, not around us, but within us. The Eye showed me: the approaching Boundless War will not be between you and I, not between them and their neighbors, but between I and I.

The clichés are true: conquer the weak I so that the mighty I can arise. Of course, being always mighty, always strong is not ideal. To propel ourselves, we must have a little weakness within. Weakness is the mortar of determination and perseverance, will is its brickwork. How well you mix the two will determine how well-built the house you call your soul will be. Will the squall of the crowd blow it over, or shall you stand—like Moses did between the ramparts of the Red Sea—head raised high, against these formidable waters of servitude to the horde.

Doom is coming. Nay, doom is already here, and every day it chips away at human will, and inches along, consuming Men of weak resolve via depression and angst and anxiety, as it did to all those who have come before us.

The Eye of Eyes. The I of I's.

What does it all mean, my friend? Which one is the true me? Is the I that goes to work each and every day, filling out paperwork and enriching my superiors, the proper I? Or is the I that does the woodwork in the cellar, the happy me, the one who harkens back to the truth of my essence? Is the I that emerges when I am with a beautiful girl the real I? Or the one that hangs around when I'm alone? Which eyes of mine see the real world? And which ones see the fictitious one?

I used to walk through the woods and think it peaceful. I became enamored with the silence of this *real world,* until, one day, I came upon a lynx killing a piglet. The blood that slicked the lynx's maw and the piglet's back awoke a primordial fear within me. Was this the reality of the world? Is the frightened eye the real eye? Is that I me? And what of relationships: is the real I the one at the start of a relationship or the one seven years in? The one who loved and cared, or the one indifferent and dispassionate? Is the real I me alone or me around people? The I is as ambiguous and liquid as a wave. It exists only for a moment, and in specific circumstances, before it's gone. That is the I—the eye.

Every person fades in the same way: slowly.

The depths of the sea, of the desert, of the wind course through me, from me, and into the world. The soundtrack of my life has been the bustle and hustle of the work place, but its closing moments are a symphony of voices from the Black Plane. A lamentation. Everything ends the same way: with a wail of silence. We enter psychological places that we're not meant to enter. We call those places dreams. As Freud wrote, "The dream often reveals to us what we do not wish to admit to ourselves, and that we, therefore, unjustly condemn it as a liar and deceiver."[53] Pain makes being a curse. But pain is, like a dream, a liar and deceiver. It hopes to makes us nihilistic, broken, angry, resentful, inhuman. Although broken, and perhaps insane, I believe that being is a blessing because it gives us a shot at the potentiality to feel the

53 Freud, 68.

truth and feign knowledge. To be is to hope. And even though, each of us knows that the end is nigh, what a splendid end it will be: Man is the only creature capable of art, and when hellfire comes, he'll sing beautiful verses of the shimmer of the flames and how they inspire true love.

I miss my parents. I miss them dearly. My mother was right, I should have lived a normal life. I should have found myself a girl, fell in love, and lived like the herd. It is too late for that now. The Eye of Eyes had showed me the schematic. Everything is designed with an ending in mind. Even Man.

Especially Man.

Sincerely, your friend,
Jan Cichy

AFTERWORD

JAN CICHY'S STORY—MEANING this letter—is an odd one, filled with too many unknowns to make a proper judgment on its actual meaning. No one knows Jan's fate. Did he commit suicide? Did he remain in Arabia? Perhaps, he returned to Europe? Or did he perish, as Dr. Zdzisława Hollender claims, in an insane asylum in Damascus?[54] There are a great many paths that lead toward each of these conclusions. Ultimately, the answers to these questions will remain unanswered. For my part, the best I can do is to provide a general outline of what we know happened, via various documents and interviews, during and after the period that Jan sent *The Eye of Eyes* to his friend, Dr. Michał Nowak.

February 5th, a day after his initial departure from Snowshill, Jan crash-landed on the Spanish cost. From an interview with the couple who first saw him—José Majorca and his, at the time, sweetheart, Sofía Elena García—we know it was the late afternoon. Mr. Majorca states that the 'balloon,' as the witnesses called it, appeared out of nowhere and quickly fell into the sea. Ms. García confirms this, adding, "There was a terrible noise. Screams and low yelps that foxes make when they are 'speaking' to one another. Then the balloon just materialized. It appeared as if

54 All translations are the my own. Hollender, Zdzisława. "Wiele Twarzy Jana Cichego." *Literatura Zapomniana*, 20 Nov. 1997, pp. 77.

reveled from under a magic blanket. Then it quickly fell. I mean, fast, like a heavy stone."[55]

There were three other witnesses: Vincent Louise, a local fisherman, Babieca Morales, an old librarian, and Raimundo Pérez, a local schoolboy. Mr. Morales notes, "I heard a roar like a bear or some sort of lion makes, followed by the balloon emerging from the blue of the sky itself."[56] The spot where the aero-craft fell is a popular sunbathing destination, but since the crash occurred in early February, the pool of witnesses was rather small. Few people wander the shore during these months.

It's important to note, that according to Jan, he was near the Icelandic coast on the morning of the fifth. Clearly, these calculations were impossible. This begs the question, why were Jan's calculations off? Either he was wrong, lying, or something quite unusual happened. How could an engineer, who takes pride in his detailed work, be off by hundreds, if not thousands, of kilometers? A mistake seems unlikely. If the objective of his journey was a latitudinal circumnavigation of the globe, then what purpose would lying have in his ultimate success? From what we can gather, fame and celebrity were not part of his mindset. Evidently, his focus lay in proving that the technology he had worked on for several years worked. Was he not confident in his creation? Perhaps. However, he states several times in *The Eye of Eyes* that he is sure of the success of his work. Finally, his tale overflows with fantasy and delusion. Did these events occur? No. Perhaps? Who knows. However, delusion and hallucination associated with schizophrenics is a potential answer. But then, how does a man who has never shown any schizophrenic tendencies in the past become so overnight? Yet another mystery. The more we analyze Jan's tale, the more inconsistencies, ambiguities, and questions we walk away

55 Baja, Antoni. *Wahnsinn und Verstand* – Rejected Article. 1921, pp. 3.

56 Ibid., 7.

with then when we first began. Because of this, *The Eye of Eyes* is a narrative ouroboros.

Mr. Majorca also noted that as the craft fell, he saw a person jump from it and into the sea. Moments later, another figure jumped. The aero-craft struck the waves, and somehow, most likely through the mere force of the impact, the balloon and the craft separated. The wind blew the balloon out onto the shore, where it became lodged between and pierced by some crags. "There were two people who jumped from the balloon, of that I'm sure," Mr. Majorca confirms.[57]

Without hesitation, Mr. Majorca dove into the water to save Jan and this secondary figure, but he saved neither of them. Jan washed ashore on his own, while the second, mysterious man never surfaced. In a 1928 interview with graduate student, Daniel Kozuch, Mr. Majorca said, "There was another man. He was struggling to stay afloat. He gave off a strange scream. A big wave crashed over us and I lost sight of him. When I swam to where he I last saw him, he was no gone. The waves must have taken him under. I believe he drowned"[58] Mr. Kozuch notes that Ms. García no longer lived in the village at the time of the interview and was not available to confirm or deny her former sweetheart's statements. However, Raimundo Pérez—27 years older at the time of the interview—notes, "I recall two people jumping from the balloon, but only one emerged from the water. The weird one with the mad eyes."[59]

Regarding Jan's emergence from the sea, Ms. García said, "I ran up to him as soon as I saw him, but he quickly stood up and was livid. He yelled about not being himself. About keeping the

57 Ibid., 18.

58 Kozuch, Daniel. "Auf Jan Cichy." *Schrecken des Geistes*, 1, Apr. 1928, pp. 13.

59 Ibid., 16.

Eye at bay. About some door. Then he ran off down the beach. I never saw him after that. And why would I want to? I thought that a madman just washed ashore. I kept my distance. José swam to shore soon after. It was horrid. He was exhausted. He almost drowned out there. For a whole week, he was ill with the cold."[60] Mr. Louise, the fisherman, told Mr. Kozuch that, "The stranger ran down the beach, but then abruptly turned toward the village. Old Guaracho, [Mr. Simon Francisco de Plazo, the old man with the mule and cart], later told me that he drove a foreigner to San Judas. He said, the man was odd, murmuring to himself along the road, but didn't seem dangerous. 'He seemed like a lost cause,' Guaracho said. 'I pitied him."[61] Mr. de Plazo passed away three years prior to Mr. Kozuch's arrival, thus it is impossible to know exactly what happened on the road to San Judas.

The aero-craft was never recovered. In the summer of 2012, I rented a boat and, along with a couple of friends, searched for the craft but, unfortunately, found nothing. One hundred and eleven years passed since the crash. The craft had either already disintegrated, or the sea floor had reclaimed it via overgrowth or sediment layering atop of it. The balloon, most likely, ended up in the trash. "I'm not sure if it was taken away by Deleminor [a local policeman] and sent to the rubbish pile outside of town, or if someone else took and reused it. Whatever happened, it's not here anymore," Ms. García said.[62]

Jan's trip homeward is also noteworthy. He states that most of the journey back to England had been a blur, but gives a list of the cities that he came across on his way back. There is no evidence to suggest that he was there, but none that he was not. Connecting all the Spanish cities, in which Jan stayed, yields a

---

60 Baja, 1921, 9

61 Kozuch, 1928, 19.

62 Baja, 1921, 12.

rather believable path home. There is no evidence as to where he entered England. Dr. Zdzisława Hollender claims that he never returned to London.[63] However, he must have because his parents received the money from the sale of his flat and the plethora of items that he sent via carrier. On the other hand, without having the address of the flat nor the names of the realtor and attorney involved, locating receipts or documents confirming the sale has been futile.

Jan sent the manuscript from Salalah, Oman. The postage and stamps upon the envelope confirm this. Thus, we know, without any doubt, that—at the very least—he did make it to the Arabian Peninsula. Unfortunately, the package intended for his friend, Dr. Nowak, never reached its intended target. Upon reaching Kraków, the package became lost in Jagiellonian University's internal mail system. By the time it surfaced, in 1920, Dr. Nowak had been dead for three years. Conscripted by the Austro-Hungarian army, he perished in the trenches at the Battle of Mărășești in Romania.

Having found the manuscript in some dusty corner, prof. Antoni Baja, intrigued by the madness of the work, wrote in an article for a short lived Polish Medical Journal, *Umysł Ludzki* [1920-1923], "The human mind is brittle. Anything—from a mistimed laugh to a prolonged glance—can bring it a breaking point. Take Jan Cichy, as example. In his rambling manuscript, circa 1901(?), he writes of his parents, bureaucracy, the unfairness of life, yet blames his maladies on something he calls the Eye of Eyes. One can presume the pressures of life made him crack. 'The Eye' was his escape, his excuse. Every person is simply trying to get what they want: a carefree life that omits contemplation and self-blame. In other words, a fantasy."[64] After a short vacation on

---

63 Hollender, 74.

64 Baja, Antoni. "Ludzki umysł i szaleństwo." *Umysł Ludzki*, 1 Feb. 1922, pp. 49.

Spanish coast, where he interviewed several witnesses, but before his piece for *Umysł Ludzki*, prof. Baja submitted an article to the German journal, *Wahnsinn und Verstand* [1913-1933]. The article was rejected on the grounds that it bordered on fantasy.

Prof. Antoni Baja notes that Jan's potential breakdown may have tricked his mind into seeing doubles of himself. He writes, "It so often happens, that an overburdened mind creates solutions to its own problems. And what is the biggest problem that any one of us has? Ourselves. The 'replicas, imitations, and doubles' that Mr. Cichy writes about are, in my opinion, projections of his own faults, evils, and insecurities. And how does he overcome them? By figuratively killing them. By going out and hunting them in the symbolic desert."[65] Prof. Baja's diagnosis is reminiscent of the syndrome of subjective doubles (SSD), classified by psychiatrist George Nikolaos Christodoulou in 1978. SSD is a delusional misidentification syndrome in which the subject experiences visions of having a Doppelgänger. The double shares the subject's appearance, but differs slightly in character and may or may not be uncanny to the subject's perception. Did Jan Cichy suffer from SSD? Perhaps, but they do not align with the strange occurrences described by Jan's mother.

During the interwar years, a young graduate student, Daniel Kozuch, read Jan's manuscript, and was so moved by it, that he traveled to Spain and the United Kingdom to interview as many people as he could who were involved in the tale. His curiosity eventually led him to Snowshill where he met Jan's mother. Unfortunately, Jan's father had passed away by then. The interview confirms that Jan had visited his parent's farm only a few days after he had supposedly sent the manuscript from Oman. Jan's mother said, "He was acting strangely. He didn't explain anything. He wasn't aware of the circumnavigation, and gave, neither me nor

65 Ibid., 53.

my husband, any explanation of what had happened to him on the adventure...When my husband confronted him about the sale of the flat, for which we got a substantial amount of money that we wanted to return to him, he knew nothing of it. He denied it and became frustrated. Throughout the whole conversation, he kept interrupting and asking us when he visited the farm last. When we told him that we haven't seen him since he flew off in February of that year, he rushed out of the door, screaming like an animal."[66]

She went on to say that both her and her husband had seen him several times at random roaming their property or stalking them through the village. When they attempted to confront him, he would simply run off. The sightings stopped in spring 1914. "We stopped seeing him after the St Martin-in-the-Fields Church bombing in London. That was sometime in April of 1914. I wept often. I mean, both of my sons abandoned me. It was heartbreaking. But after my husband died, I reflected on the last time I spoke with Jan, about the chilling way he watched us from the distance. I know now what I felt then, that whoever that was, he wasn't my son. Mother's intuition, I guess. The man who flew off in 1901 never returned and that makes me very sad."[67]

Mr. Kozuch intended to write his doctoral dissertation about madness and literature with Jan Cichy's manuscript as its centerpiece. However, he abandoned the idea. His notes from the time (provided by the generosity of his great-great grandchild, Maria Walkoszka) state, "Hołomisz [Mr. Kozuch's doctoral adviser] advises against perusing the Cichy manuscript any further. He said it's all rubbish and fantasy. 'This is the new age. We must cast away superstitions and foolishness for a better future: the mechanical, the scientific. Write about literature of the advancement of human

66 Kozuch, Daniel. Unpublished and discarded PhD Notes from Personal Notebooks, 1927, pp. 97.

67 Kozuch, 1927, 99.

ingenuity, not about some rustic lunatic,' he said. He's right. It's best to look at some *fin de siècle*,[68] perhaps Machen's *The Great God Pan*[69] contrasted against the works of H.G. Wells. A few beers will show me the way."[70] With *The Eye of Eyes* abandoned, Mr. Kozuch gave the work a last *hoorah* by submitting an article about it and its author to the German fantasy magazine, *Schrecken des Geistes* [1925-1933]. He concluded his piece thus, "Other worlds lay hidden just under the layers of space and time that our fragile biological frames don't allow us to see. There exists more beyond the unperceivable than our science can uncover. Perchance, Jan Cichy ventured into this line between everything and the abyss, and when he reemerged, part of it clung onto him like a tick does to a Man who goes venturing into the unexplored thicket."[71]

Jan Cichy's fate is a mystery. However, we know of at least two people who have seen him before his disappearance. One of whom was Thomas Swade-Owen, Jan's workmate from the patent bureau. Mr. Kozuch notes, "When I brought up Jan Cichy to Mr. Swade-Owen, the man became very angry. He did not wish to discuss him, but mentioned that the strange fellow used to stalking him for several years, but suddenly stopped just before the outbreak of the War. I did not pursue the subject further."[72] After a great deal of patience in ancient Turkish libraries and historical societies, Dr. Zdzisława Hollender uncovered an old Ottoman 'permit of entrance' into the Empire, dated March 13, 1901, made out to Janusz Cichy by border guard, Yusuf Özdemir. A copy is

68 French for "end of century." Often associated with literature and art. The term references the closing of one era and onset of another, typically used to refer to the end of the 19th century, a period of degeneracy and, simultaneous, hope for a new beginning.

69 A horror/fantasy novella written by Welsh author, Arthur Machen.

70 Kozuch, 1927, 63.

71 Kozuch, 1928, 19.

72 Ibid., 22.

filed in Istanbul's Historical Society office.[73] However, instead of clarifying Cichy's travels, the permit creates even more questions. How could he have traveled outside continental Europe, be stalking his parents in Snowshill and his colleague in London, all the while, sending packages from Oman in the span of a few weeks? Remember, this is before the invention of the jet engine.

Hitler must have read the Mr. Kozuch's *Schrecken des Geistes* article and became interested in Jan Cichy's manuscript because he gave a direct order to Alfred Rosenberg,[74] the Reich's head of the Ministry for the Occupied Eastern Territories (1941–1945), and rumored head of the Führer's secret Bureau on Occult Matters, that when Kraków fell, the manuscript was to be deliver to him, personally. When Poland fell on October 6, 1939, the Nazis raided Jagiellonian University's libraries. The Cichy Manuscript disappeared. From historical documents we know, Hitler never received it.[75] Tried in Nuremburg after the War, Rosenburg was hung in 1946, and all knowledge of *The Eye of Eyes* was lost. However, in 1976 when one of Rosenburg's undocumented properties went up for sale, the manuscript was rediscovered in a hidden safe, and promptly returned to the Jagiellonian University Library, where it sat unread among numerous tomes until 1997, when Dr. Hollender and I stumbled upon it by chance.

As of this writing, the manuscript sits in Jagiellonian University Library's archives. However, since 2019 it is only available for viewing via written permission from the University's Rector. Bizarrely, Jan mentions that he lost the Saint Christopher medallion that his mother had given him, but it is among the things found in the manuscript file. I know, because I've had the privilege

73 Hollender, 79.

74 Gefälscht, Gert. *Dieses Buch ist nicht echt*. Munich, Gunder and Flunder, 1989, pp. 217.

75 Ibid., 219.

of rereading Jan's work as late as September 2020. Yet another mystery emerges.

In the end, *The Eye of Eyes* is a strange tale that plays with both facts and fiction. One can read it over and over again, and walk away noticing different details and symbolisms after each reading. This makes the manuscript a fascinating example of literary madness meeting pop fantasy. What I wouldn't give to sit down with its author over a cup of coffee and discuss its madness?

Mirosław Słowik

Lisbon, 2021

Jan Cichy (1864-1901?) was born in Wzrokienice, Poland. During his lifetime he was an inventor, engineer, patent officer, and aviation pioneer. He spent the latter part of his life in-between London and Snowshill, England. In 1901, he ventured on a latitudinal circumnavigation of the globe. It is unknown what happened to him.

Mirosław Słowik was born in Warsaw, Poland and now lives in-between Kraków and Minneapolis. He is retired, but works as a part-time lecturer of linguistic anthropology at Hollowday Academy. He has authored over 200 articles and essays.

Adam Zmarzlinski was born in the Tatra Mountains and now lives near Chicago. He is in the process of finishing a Ph.D. Among his various honors are the Michał Heller Prize, Amnesty International's "Moral for a Dictator" Human Rights Fairy Tale Award, and the Marilyn Houghton Keyton Founder's Prize for Poetry.

ALSO FROM MONOTREME PRESS

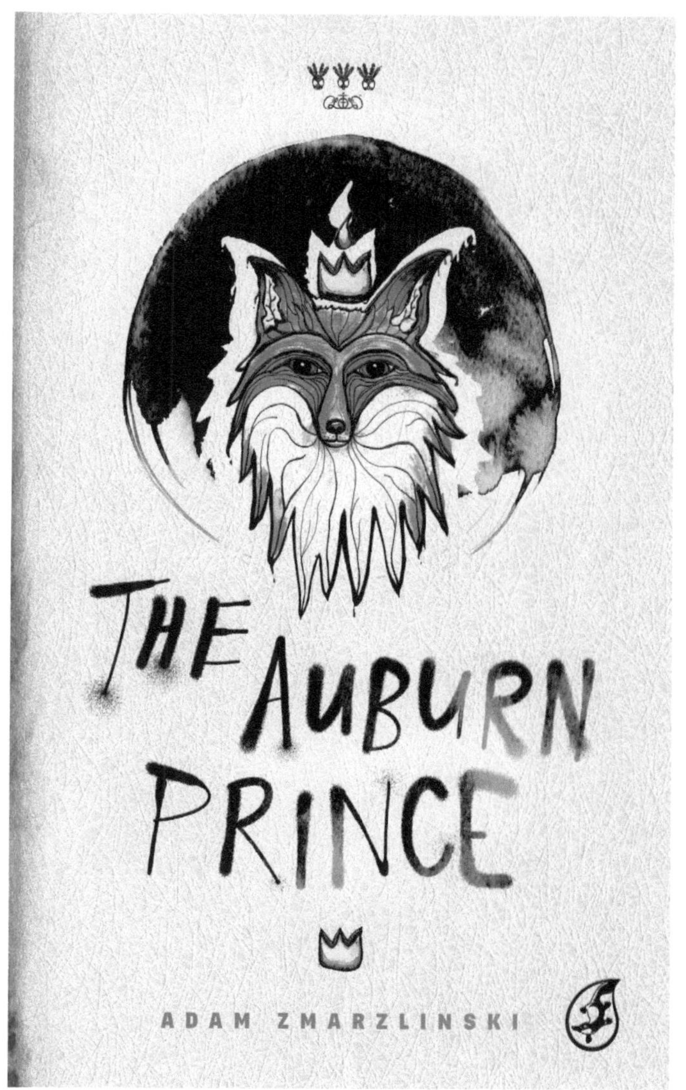

www.ingramcontent.com/pod-product-compliance
Lightning Source LLC
Chambersburg PA
CBHW030531310726
48979CB00010B/1879/J

* 9 7 8 1 9 5 1 3 2 6 0 2 9 *